一隻小犬

ONE
SMALL
DOG

一隻小犬

ONE
SMALL
DOG

BY S. T. TUNG

董時進著

ILLUSTRATED BY TED LEWIN

DODD, MEAD & COMPANY, NEW YORK

BL/6

Library of Congress Cataloging in Publication Data

Tung, S T
   One small dog.

   SUMMARY: When a campaign is initiated during
the 1950's to annihilate the dogs of China as a famine-
fighting measure, a boy tries to save his little dog.
   [1. China—Fiction] I. Lewin, Ted, ill. II. Title.
PZ7.T82330n   [Fic]   74–25525
ISBN 0–396–07122–8

AUTHOR'S
FOREWORD

一隻小犬

Foreign visitors to China have reported that there
are no dogs in that country. This is because all canines were killed in the mid-fifties when the Communists ordered a nationwide campaign to annihilate the dogs of China. Not only dogs, but cats,
sparrows, and rats were objects of government attention in an effort to save food for the people. The
campaigns were drastic measures but seemed necessary in the face of famine.

1 New Market Place is no longer new. It was built more than a hundred years ago but still retains the name given it at its birth. There is still only a single narrow street, neatly paved with flagstones quarried from a nearby hill. In the beginning the street was about a hundred paces long; since then as many new houses have been added to the ends of the street as were there at first. The houses are all connected, sharing walls. Regardless of the time they were built, they are all of the same height, shape, and color, and of the same material—posts of small pines and walls of white-plastered, woven bamboo splinters. The only exceptions are the brick temples.

One temple at the end of the street stands out more prominently than the others. This is Yui-wang-kung, dedicated to an ancient emperor and engineer who lived forty centuries ago and is still remembered for his achievements in flood control. The temple has a large courtyard with the shrines in the back, a theatrical stage in the front, and a double-roofed tower in the middle. These roofs curve upward at the corners, each corner with a spire at the end, and there is a taller spire in the middle of the top roof. All the spires are inlaid with broken pieces of painted chinaware, so that they sparkle in the sun.

Our story begins here one late afternoon in early summer. It was a hot and sultry day, typical of the weather of that time of the year in south-central China. The sun had nearly completed the day's journey, but the heat still lingered. Loud, ear-piercing noises floated out from the courtyard of the temple into the quiet village. A group of boys playing soccer had only a green, unripe shaddock for a ball. As they kicked the thick-rinded citrus fruit back and forth with their bare feet, they kept shouting at the top of their voices. Sweat was streaming down their reddened faces and bare bodies, which they wiped with their dirty hands, scattering the water on the paving stones.

Nipping playfully at their bare feet and the shaddock was a half-grown puppy. It had coal-black fur, white paws, and a white-tipped tail. Running about and barking joyfully, it tried to seize the shaddock with its paws and jaws.

"Get out of the way, Lucky, we might step on you," a lean-faced and slender-limbed lad said to the dog, and he led it away to the edge of the court. The only boy who had not been shouting and screaming, he ran after the ball quietly, his face serious as

8

though his mind was deeply absorbed in the game. His large, eager eyes were bright and quick, his features clear cut. His name was Sung, which means pine tree in Chinese.

Lucky sat down where his owner commanded him, on the edge of the terrace beside the courtyard, in front of one of the black-lacquered coffins stored there on low benches by a coffin maker. He watched the boys with a cocked head and an eager face. It was apparent that he itched to return to the game, but he was an obedient dog.

The dusk was approaching so the boys stopped playing and abandoned the battered shaddock in the middle of the yard. Sung picked up his faded blue shirt from a bench near Lucky and was wiping his face and ribs with it when suddenly a pack of dogs, their tails between their legs, flew into the temple and scuttled into hiding places. At their heels were several uniformed men carrying spears and shotguns that flashed dazzlingly in the setting sun.

"Where have they gone?" the men demanded as they dashed across the courtyard and up the stone steps toward the main building which housed the deity's image. No one replied.

Sung understood at once what was happening— the long-rumored Annihilate-the-Dogs Campaign had begun in New Market Place! He acted quickly, pushing Lucky under the nearest coffin and throwing his shirt over him.

"Be quiet," he commanded in a low and stern

voice. "You are in danger. They are the dog hunters. They want to kill all the dogs." He sat down in front of the coffin to try to keep Lucky out of sight.

Presently the terrible sound of the barking and yelping of the dogs was heard from all sides. There were several gunshots, which filled the large temple with echoes and mingled with the cursing and laughing voices of the hunters. Lucky whimpered

11

like a sick child and crawled closer to Sung.

"Be quiet," Sung ordered again in a whisper and pushed Lucky back underneath the coffin. His voice was so anguished that Lucky remained as still as the coffin.

A few minutes later, the soft, furry corpses of the slain canines were dragged by their hind legs through the courtyard by the laughing and triumphant militia. Sung counted eight bodies of different colors and sizes. He involuntarily shut his eyes and turned his head away.

When he opened his eyes again, the other boys had gone. The courtyard was abandoned, but Sung remained sitting on the terrace, leaning his back against the coffin. Should the dog hunters come back and ask him why he was there all alone and doing nothing, what would he say to them? He did not know. Fortunately, no one entered the court. Sung waited until the day had grown dark. An old, stoop-backed monk emerged from a room behind the deity's image, carrying a bundle of lighted incense sticks that sprinkled tiny sparks as he shuffled along. He planted them in a bowl of ashes before the deity and struck the *ching*, a large bowl-shaped bell, three times with a wooden stick to announce the end of day and the beginning of night. Sung glanced quickly around. No one else was in sight. He picked up his shirt and said to Lucky, "We can go home now."

Lucky crawled out from under the coffin and shook the dust from his fur, not vigorously, as he would ordinarily do, but feebly. Then he wagged his tail timidly and looked at Sung with an inquiring face.

"We can go home now," Sung repeated in a louder voice. He picked up Lucky in his arms and tiptoed across the courtyard with him. At the gate he stopped, and sticking out a cautious head, looked left and right. The street was deserted and dark, except for faint shafts of light peeping out here and there from crevices in the walls and doors.

"We are safe," he assured Lucky, and put the dog down outside the stone doorsill. Then they ran home quickly.

2 Sung had come into the possession of Lucky accidentally about four months earlier. On a chilly February morning, the boy had accompanied his father to the New Market Place to sell cabbages and spinach. When they had sold the vegetables and were going home with the empty baskets on their backs and a pack of dirty and torn *jen-min-pi*, or paper money, in a cloth bag, they saw three little puppies on the roadside just outside the village. The puppies were groping about aimlessly and whining.

"Poor little things!" Sung said to them and, bending down, fondly stroked the back of a black puppy with white paws and a white-tipped tail. "Your master has abandoned you, and you are without a mother and a home."

The little dog wagged its tiny tail, wriggled its chubby body, and licked Sung's hands.

"Poor thing!" Sung repeated. He stroked the puppy once more and resumed his journey, following his father.

To his astonishment, when he had gone about twenty or thirty paces, he discovered that the black puppy was at his heels, trotting noiselessly on its little paws. Sung waved it to go away, but the tiny creature refused to leave him. Being a dog lover, Sung was secretly rejoicing, so instead of driving the puppy away, he gave it inviting signals as he walked along.

Sung's father did not notice the dog until they had arrived at their front yard, when the puppy darted forward and ran after several chickens, scattering them and making them cackle.

"Did you bring the dog home, Sung?" his father asked in surprise.

"No, it came by itself."

"Bring it back to the village," his father commanded in a stern voice. "You know that we have nothing to feed it, because our food ration is hardly enough for ourselves."

"It can't eat much, Father, it's so small."

"But it will eat more as it grows bigger."

Sung knew that it would not do to argue with his father, so he caught the puppy to carry it back to New Market Place. Just as he reached the edge of the front yard, where a large shaddock tree stood with several of last year's fruits still unpicked, he heard his mother's voice: "Sung, were you saying that a dog had come to our house?"

"Yes, here it is," Sung replied, and rubbed his cheek against the small head. "Three puppies were abandoned outside the village. This one just ran

15

after me and I couldn't drive it away."

"Did it really? They say that a dog coming to one's home brings good luck."

"Yes, of course! That's what everybody says. Maybe this little dog will bring us luck."

"Is it a male or a female? I wouldn't want to keep a female dog, though."

"It's a male. No mistake."

Thus the puppy was accepted into the family. Right then and there, Sung's mother gave it a name —Lucky.

Everyone in the family loved Lucky and shared food with him. The little fellow grew fast. He was both handsome and intelligent. His black hair shone like lacquer; his paws and the tip of his tail were white as snow. Unlike most dogs in China, which barked at every stranger even against the order of their masters, Lucky was extraordinarily obedient and friendly. And fortunately so! Otherwise, he would have been discovered and killed by the dog hunters at Yui-wang-kung temple.

However, the Annihilate-the-Dogs Campaign had just begun, and in the days to come Sung was often to wonder whether the old popular saying that the dog brings good luck was so, or if the opposite was the truth.

3 On the market day after the dog-hunting incident at Yui-wang-kung, Sung was sauntering
along the street of New Market Place, stopping now
and then to read the posters on the wooden uprights
and white-plastered walls of the houses. They were
of many colors—red, yellow, white, green, purple.
Written on them in large characters were slogans re-
lating to the campaign: "Kill the dogs and save food
for the people"; "Dogs' meat is delicious"; "Dogs
bite people and litter the street"; "Dogs are the
spreaders of rabies"; "Dogs are the servants of the
rich and the enemy of the poor"; "Obey Chairman
Mao's order and kill off the dogs."

On the brick walls and massive doors of the temples were posted large colored pictures, crudely
drawn, showing how wicked dogs were. Some
showed them biting little beggar boys and tearing
their ragged clothes, or even digging into graves and

狗肉味美

犬是富人的僕役

富人的死敵

狗侍染狂犬病

服從毛主席
殺盡一切犬類

devouring human corpses. Sung was scanning the pictures outside Yui-wang-kung when he heard the loud sound of a gong coming from a nearby teahouse. He followed the marketers toward the source of the sound. A sizable crowd had collected in front of the teahouse, eagerness on their faces as they waited in silence. A small, bony, elderly man, whom Sung recognized as the town crier, mounted a table with the gong under his arm and, in a high-pitched voice, announced, "The commissar from the city! He will give you instructions about the Annihilate-the-Dogs Campaign."

The commissar, a young man of about twenty, was wearing a new blue tunic and visored cap. He was diminutive in stature and grave in appearance. He climbed on the table and stood still for half a minute, surveying the crowd left and right. Then he began speaking through a large tin trumpet. His voice was loud and piercing, and as he spoke he shook his fists unceasingly. What he said repeated and explained the slogans on the posters. Then he announced that he had eaten dog meat many times and loved it more and more. As he said this and smacked his lips, the crowd burst into laughter. The commissar's face became stern and angry, and the audience stopped laughing.

When the official had concluded his speech, paper banners attached to little bamboo sticks were distributed to the crowd by his assistants, and a parade started with the commissar leading the way. Sung was caught in the stream of bare-legged men wearing large *tsao mao*, or straw hats, and straw sandals. They marched in comical goosesteps, shouting slogans in shrill and discordant voices and waving the colorful banners. Sung plodded along with closed lips. As soon as they reached the end of the street, the men turned back and marched in the opposite direction. There were deserters from time to time, so that when they arrived at Yui-wang-kung and were dismissed, the column had shortened to about half its original length.

Sung sat down on the stone steps outside the big temple, his palms supporting his chin and his elbows resting on his knees. He was thinking of Lucky and how the little dog would probably run to greet the soldiers coming to kill him, and he was wondering how he could save his dog when he felt a hand on his shoulder and heard, "What are you doing here all alone, my boy?"

Sung turned and looked up at a towering figure in a tight-fitting tunic, under which muscles seemed bursting. It was a moment before he recognized the man and cried out, "It's Uncle Ching Chang! Why are you wearing an official uniform?"

"I'm a sort of official," Ching Chang, who was no relative but was pleased by the honorable greeting, replied with a chuckle and an air of importance. "I work for the government now, and I've just come home from a mission to a far place in the south."

Ching Chang was a large man with dark, uncomely features, but his bulk, combined with a throaty and resonant voice, made him impressive, sometimes even awe-inspiring. He had a protruding chin, and on its right side was a black pea-sized wart, from which a coarse hair shot forth like a bristle. He had formed the habit of twirling that hair whenever he was confronted with a problem. He had been a peddler of pigs, buying from places where they were abundant and cheap and driving them to places where they were scarce and dear. Recently, he said, he had found a job with the local *hsien*, or county, government, transporting small pigs to the coastal districts in the vicinity of Canton.

"But what are you doing here all alone?" Ching Chang repeated. "Why don't you come with me to Wu's eating house to have a bowl of noodles? I'm terribly thirsty and hungry. You see, I've just returned from an official trip to the south and have not put anything into my mouth all morning."

"I'm just resting after the long march," Sung said. "But I must go home now." He was filled with anxiety for Lucky's fate and had no appetite for anything. He thanked Ching Chang and plodded home with bent head and gloomy face, the commissar's words and the shouted slogans ringing in his ears.

His mother met him at the threshold and asked, "What is the matter? Are you sick?" And she put a hand to his temple to test his temperature.

"No." Then he told her what he had seen and heard at New Market Place.

His mother sighed and said, "I think they will spare the dogs of the farms, because they are useful for keeping watch against thieves."

It appeared that her conjecture was right, for in the days that followed, nothing more was heard about the dog-hunting campaign, and dogs were seen running around the farmhouses and on the levees of paddy fields unhampered. Then, just as Sung's heart had been set at rest, he received shocking news. On a late afternoon, after several days of intermittent rain, he returned home from the hillsides almost submerged by the overflowing basket of green, succulent grass he carried on his back, Lucky trotting before him. Suddenly Lucky started to run. Sung raised his head and saw his mother beckoning to the dog from the edge of the threshing yard beside the shaddock tree. When Lucky reached her, she quickly picked him up and ran toward the house.

"What is the matter, Mother?" Sung shouted.

"I'll tell you," she replied from the door of the kitchen.

Sung carried the grass to the buffalo shed in the back of the house and emptied it beside a pile of dry rice straw that the buffalo was munching. Then he ran to the kitchen. "What is it? Where have you put Lucky?" he asked his mother.

She bent close to him and said in a whisper, "I've locked him in your room." She paused a moment before she went on, "Two militiamen were here a while ago. They asked me whether we have any dogs in our home."

"No!" Sung cried. "What did you say to them?"

She smiled, and her eyes twinkled meaningfully, almost mischievously, as she replied, "I said, 'Well, if I say no, you may not believe me, but if I say yes, I shan't be able to produce one. You may come in and look for yourselves.' "

"Did they search the house?"

"No. They only looked in from the door. Then one of them said, 'You are aware that it is Chairman Mao's orders that all the dogs in our country must be killed to save food for the people?' I said, 'Yes, I'm aware of that.' The other man said, 'You understand that you'll be penalized if you are found to have a dog in your home after this day?' I said, 'Yes, I understand.' Then they went away."

Sung looked at her admiringly for a moment. But then the fear rushed in.

"You've been tactful, Mother," Sung commended. "But what shall we do with Lucky? How are we going to save him?"

"And ourselves?" added his mother. "Remember what the militiamen said? We will be punished besides."

Sung heaved a sigh and groaned. He sat down on one of the long, narrow benches at the square dining table, and both mother and son were quiet. They remained so until Sung's father came home from New Market Place. As he tossed the empty baskets on the floor, he blurted out vehemently, "I saw something that made me nauseated. In the front yard of Yui-wang-kung they had built two large stoves with broken bricks and stones and set two huge cauldrons on them. What do you think they were doing with them? Cooking dog flesh!"

"They cooked dogs right in front of a sacred temple!" Sung's mother cried. "Do they really eat dog meat?"

"They both eat it and sell it."

"Who are they?" Sung cried, wanting to smash

the men who could eat dogs.

"The militia and soldiers, of course. They munched with relish and smacked their lips loudly to entice customers. 'Ah, delicious! Tender! Come on, try some,' they said to the lookers-on. I could see some mouths watering. But most turned away, shaking their heads and muttering, 'Abominable.'"

"Outrageous! Eating dog flesh; I never heard of it before." Sung's mother kept groaning as she trotted back and forth between the stove and the table.

Her husband lit his long bamboo pipe with a cornstalk from the stove and, puffing, went on, "Li's butcher shop has reopened after having been closed down for two months because there was neither pork nor mutton to sell. Today the butcher's table is piled with meat, with two horns and two hoofs of a goat hung on a rack beside it. Everybody knows that only the horns and hoofs belong to the goat but the meat belongs to the dogs."

"Are the customers fooled?" asked his wife.

"Lots of people buy the meat. I'm sure that they know what it is they are buying, but they pretend that it is goat meat. You see, the price is so cheap, and everybody is starving for meat because they have not had any for so long."

"I understand. But please don't ever bring any to your home. I simply will not cook it."

"I'll throw it in the gutter, in the manure pit," Sung blurted out vehemently.

That night Sung could hardly fall asleep for worrying about Lucky.

4 Dog-hunting was soon undertaken on a larger scale. The militiamen enlisted volunteers to assist them. They scoured the countryside, besieged farmhouses and hamlets, and ransacked kitchens and bedrooms in search of dogs. They made strange noises around the houses, imitated dogs' barks and howls, and used dogs' bones to decoy them.

Strange to say, the dogs seemed to have learned to be wise. When they saw strangers come near the house, they would not bark as they used to but would quietly retreat to some hiding place, such as stacks of stalks, the empty space under the bins, or the rice fields around the houses.

"Ah, what kind of world are we living in!" Sung's mother lamented with a deep sigh, when they were telling each other stories about the dog-hunting. "Isn't the home the dog's sacred retreat, upon which no strangers may trespass? But now the dog is being hunted and killed right in its own home."

"You speak of sacred retreats for dogs," her husband retorted. "Do people have retreats nowadays?"

"I know." She gave another deep sigh. "I wonder how much longer we can protect Lucky. We have to keep him out of sight all the time."

"And out of hearing, too," her husband said.

From that day, Lucky was shut inside the house most of the time. Sung's mother would take care that the little black dog was quiet whenever there were strangers around. Should the hunters appear in the front, she would lead Lucky out through the back door, and vice versa. The paddy fields all around the house provided a convenient sanctuary where Lucky could hide in case of emergency. But as the rice was ripening and would soon be cut, Sung's worry deepened. He became irritable, thinking about a place to hide Lucky.

Then a formal edict was proclaimed by the magistrate of the county, requiring all dog owners voluntarily to surrender their dogs or be subject to heavy punishment. When Sung learned the news from his father that evening, he clenched both fists and vowed, "I will never, never surrender Lucky, no matter what happens."

"I don't see how we can get away with it if you don't," his father said. "He'll be discovered sooner or later. If he is found after the time limit, not only will he be killed, but we shall be punished besides."

"I'll take him to some other place."

"To what other place?"

"Where they don't kill dogs."

"There's no such place in the whole country. It is the policy of the Central Government to kill off all the dogs, don't you understand?"

"I'll take him to the deep mountains and hide him in the forest."

His father gave a loud guffaw. "You want to make him a guerrilla? But how is he going to live in the mountains and forest? Who is going to feed him?"

Sung made no reply; he did not know what to say.

His father went on, "Perhaps he could hunt his food, but I doubt he can catch enough. Not only that, but how are you going to get rid of him in the first place? You can take him to the mountains, but he'll follow you when you come home. Even if you could hide from him, he could find his way home. Then he would be discovered by the dog hunters and be killed anyway."

For the first time Sung appreciated fully the difficulty of his problem. He felt as if he were locked inside a cellar that admitted neither light nor air. He had no appetite for his supper and ate only half the rice he usually did. Then he retired to his room and went to bed. After a short sleep, he woke from a bad dream. He lay on his back with eyes wide open. The night was so quiet he could hear Lucky breathe beside the bed. He was aware of the absence of the barking of the neighborhood dogs that had been so common in the past.

After lying there thinking for about half an hour, he suddenly jumped out of bed and tiptoed to his parents' room. He knew they were not asleep, because the light was still on. He tapped on the door and said, "May I have a word with you, Mother?"

His mother opened the door a crack, and said, "What is it?" She had been sewing before a dim kerosene lamp.

"Is Uncle Ching Chang going to take another drove of pigs to Canton for the government?" Sung asked in a low voice.

"Why? Did you get up at this hour just to ask me that? What if he is? What if he is not? Maybe he has left already."

"He has not," Sung's father put in from the bed, poking his head out of the quilt. "I saw him at New Market Place this morning. But how does that interest you so much that you must find it out at this time?"

Instead of answering his father's question, Sung asked, "How far is Canton from Hong Kong?"

His father sat up and demanded, "But why? Why are you asking all these questions?"

"Please tell me, it's important," Sung beseeched.

"It is not far, just four or five hours by train. But I insist, why do you want to know such things? What are you up to?"

Sung still ignored his father's question and persisted, "Is Hong Kong a safe place? I mean, do they kill dogs there?"

His father burst into a laugh and cried, "I see! I see what you are after. You want to send Lucky to Hong Kong, isn't that it?"

"Yes, that's the only way to save him. Lots of people have fled to Hong Kong. Why can't dogs do the same?"

"Well, I don't think they kill dogs in Hong Kong," Sung's father said. "But how can Lucky get there? He'd be discovered and killed as soon as he got outside this house. Besides, a dog must have a home, a master or mistress, otherwise he would starve. We don't know anybody in Hong Kong, so even if you could bring Lucky there safely, which I doubt very much, it would amount to sending him to a starvation camp."

Sung not only had considered these problems but thought that he had found their solution. He would travel with Ching Chang and his herd of little pigs. The pigs were black, and so was Lucky; they were about the same size. So, thought Sung, it wouldn't be too difficult to smuggle Lucky in a large herd of pigs. As for a master or mistress in Hong Kong, why, Lucky was such a lovely dog, anyone would pick him up and bring him home. But Sung did not mention these thoughts to his parents; he only asked, "Will you allow me to go to Canton with Uncle Ching Chang?"

"I don't care," his father replied. "It may be a good chance for you to see a big city if he allows you to travel with him. You had better go to speak to him in the morning." Then he lay down and pulled the quilt over him.

Sung put his mouth to his mother's ear and said,

"Will you come to my room so we don't have to disturb Father?"

His mother followed him across the middle room. Lucky, who had been sleeping on the floor before Sung's bed, got up, stretched his legs, and wagged his whole body to his mistress as if he had missed her for a long time.

Mother and son sat down on the bed, and she put a hand on Lucky's head and stroked it. Then Sung began:

"I . . . I must . . . must have some . . . money to make the trip to Hong Kong, but . . ." He stopped short.

"How much do you need?" his mother asked.

"I don't know, but I guess maybe several *yuan*."

"All I have is forty coppers left from the egg money. I've spent some for a piece of cloth to make slippers, which I am working on now."

"Will father give me the money?"

"He doesn't have any money. He is more hard pressed now than ever with the tax so heavy and the price of vegetables so low."

"Then, I won't be able to make the trip," Sung said, "and Lucky will be killed like the other dogs."

Sung's mother put her head in her hands and said, "What can we do?"

For a full minute mother and son sat side by side and not a word passed between them. Sung felt he would cry, but he bit his lips and fought back his tears. Lucky, as if he had been scolded, drooped his head and tail, circled, and lay down on the floor before the bed, with eyes wide open and ears pricked up as though awaiting his fate.

At last Sung's mother broke the silence and said, "I'll tell you what I can do. I can give you my hairpin. It's made of silver, weighing almost an ounce, and it is of exquisite workmanship. I will also give you all my coppers." She reached up to the back of her head, unfastened the hairpin from her bun, and laid the pin on the quilt.

Sung fastened his eyes on the shining object and felt the tears rising behind them. At last he said, "But, Mother, you must have the pin to hold your hair in place." He choked as he spoke.

"I have another one, made of bamboo," his mother said, making an effort to be cheerful. "No one does much visiting nowadays, anyway, so a bamboo hairpin serves just as well."

Sung gazed into his mother's face for several moments, then buried his head in her lap and moaned, "Oh, Mother! What a kind and generous mother!" His eyes were wet when he raised his head again.

After his mother had returned to her room, Sung held the silver pin to the lamp and admired it. It was, of course, a familiar object, which had gleamed in his mother's black bun ever since he could remember, but he had never inspected it so closely. It was the first time he had appreciated the beautiful design of chrysanthemum patterns engraved on it. He hated to see his mother part with it, because he knew how much she treasured it, but it was to be used for saving Lucky's life. He felt both happy and sad, not knowing whether he was more happy than sad, or more sad than happy. He opened the drawer of the little table, put the silver hairpin in it, then blew out the lamp and slipped under the quilt. He went to sleep almost immediately, happily unaware how inadequate the hairpin plus forty coppers were for paying for a trip to Canton and Hong Kong. He slept soundly and had many sweet dreams—the scenes and things he had heard about Hong Kong from travelers were presented to him, helter-skelter. He witnessed the sky-piercing houses built of gold and silver, and rubbed shoulders with strange crowds in bizarre attire. Many people offered to buy Lucky and pay a hundred dollars, five hundred, even a thousand. Too many people wanted to buy Lucky, so Sung did not sell him to anyone. He clung to the dream for a long time after he awoke.

The following morning Sung got up in exultant spirits just in time for breakfast. He had found a way to save Lucky. The only hurdle he had to over-come was to convince Ching Chang to accept him as a fellow traveler and cooperate with him in hiding Lucky among his pigs. Sung ate his breakfast of rice and fresh broad beans quickly, then promptly set out for Ching Chang's house.

5 Ching Chang listened to Sung attentively, half-closing his eyes, slowly twirling the bristly hair on his protruding chin and tightly compressing his lips. When Sung finished, Ching Chang put a hand on his shoulder and said in an amicable manner, "All right, my boy, I shall be delighted to have you for company. You see, I have more than a hundred little pigs to take care of. I have only two coolies to assist me, and they must look after the oxen, which carry the feed for the pigs as well as for themselves."

He took his hand from Sung's shoulder and went on, "I must make it clear right now, though, that I cannot pay you any wage. All I can do for you will be to pay for your food and lodging."

Sung almost jumped in exuberance. He wouldn't need any money to make the trip. Ching Chang would pay for his food and lodging during travel! That was beyond his wildest dream. He made a strenuous effort to hide his excitement and said,

"That's all right. You don't have to pay me any wages. I will do what I can to help you but please tell me whether Lucky will be safe!"

Ching Chang reflected for a few moments before he answered, "Well, that's difficult to say. You know that the militia and soldiers will kill any dog they catch sight of."

Sung felt a chill run down his spine and his face paled. "If Lucky's safety has no assurance, why should I make the trip?" he said.

"That's up to you," Ching Chang said resignedly. "Can't you conceal him, keep him out of sight?"

"But how?"

"Well, put him in a sack, put the sack in a basket, and carry the basket on your back."

"Are you jesting?" Sung cried, jumping up from the bench where the two were sitting. "He is not a pumpkin. How can he stay quietly in a sack? Besides, he's heavy. I can't possibly carry him all the way to Canton and Hong Kong."

Ching Chang shrugged his thick shoulders and said, "What else can you do?"

"I'm asking you. You are an official. Can't you protect one small dog?"

Ching Chang shrugged again. "It's Chairman Mao's order, and I'm only the smallest of officials, sesame-sized, as they say." He also rose from the bench and began to pace the earthen floor, back and forth, kicking at straws and twigs.

He made a dozen trips to and fro, then stopped before Sung and said, "Maybe you don't have to hide him. Maybe I *can* protect him. Suppose I tell the dog hunters that I have to have the dog to help me manage the pigs? Yes, of course!" Ching Chang suddenly raised his voice and his plain features beamed in a superior smile. "I need the dog as much as a shepherd would. The dog would also be doing an official duty. No one would dare to harm a hair on his head!"

"Wonderful!" Sung cried. And the two grasped hands to congratulate each other.

Sung ran and skipped home, happy as a smiling Buddha. He found his mother on the stone-lined earthen terrace outside the kitchen, washing clothes in a large, round wooden tub. She raised her head and spoke first. "Ah, I see you are in good spirit, you must have gotten Uncle Ching Chang's permission to go along."

"Yes, Mother," Sung replied, without stopping. He ran to his room, ignoring Lucky's warm gestures of greeting. He opened the drawer of the small table, took out the silver hairpin, ran back to his mother, unfastened the bamboo hairpin from her bun, and stuck the silver pin into the shining black knot.

"What are you doing with my hair?" his mother cried.

"I'm putting your silver pin back where it belongs," Sung said. "I have no need for it now. Here is your bamboo pin." He tossed it in the tub, and it floated for a moment, then dropped and disappeared in the darkish water.

It was not until late in the afternoon when Sung had calmed down from the excitement that he began to worry about Ching Chang's ability to protect Lucky. The dog hunters were not easy to deal with, especially now that meat was getting more scarce and dogs more rare. It may not be a bad idea, thought Sung, to accustom Lucky to a sack, so that if necessary, when passing through towns and villages, he could be carried in a basket. So the boy asked his mother to give him a large fiber sack that had been emptied of rice, took it to his room, and shut the door. He held the mouth of the sack wide open before Lucky and tried to persuade the little dog to enter.

Lucky gazed at Sung and the sack, winked an eye, and refused to budge.

"Go in, be a good dog," Sung coaxed, and held the sack closer to Lucky. But Lucky drew back. As Sung moved forward with the sack, Lucky retreated. When Lucky was completely sheltered under the bed, no amount of cajoling could induce him to come out. It was the first time that Lucky had disobeyed Sung, and the boy threw the sack on the floor, sat down on the bed, and folded his hands. A minute or two later, an idea popped up in his head.

He shuffled to the kitchen and returned with a handful of cooked rice mixed with a little lard and squeezed into a ball. Using this as bait, he succeeded in luring Lucky out from under the bed. He was planning to put the rice ball inside the sack and tempt Lucky to go in and get it, thus trapping him.

But Lucky was smart and quick; he snatched the rice ball from Sung's hand and gulped it down. Sung gave Lucky a slap and sat down again on the bed, trying to solve the problem. Lucky sat down and stared at Sung intently, apparently asking if he had more rice balls.

"I must leash him," Sung at last said to himself, "so that he cannot run wild. That's the best I can do." But Lucky had never had a leash on. In fact, Sung had never seen a leashed dog anywhere. But he knew he must teach Lucky to accept the leash before they began the journey.

Sung went to the storeroom and untied a rope from a large rice basket. Then he held Lucky between his legs and tied the rope on his neck. The little dog did not resist. However, when Sung tried to lead him, Lucky wouldn't move a step. Sung pulled harder, and Lucky dropped flat on the floor. When the boy finally threw up his hands and gave up with a sigh, Lucky tried to shake off the rope. He clawed it and bit it; finally he also gave up and trotted out of the room with a drooping tail, dragging the rope in his wake. However, he was less and less bothered by it as time went on. By the day the journey to Canton started, Lucky had grown completely used to the leash. Sung thought that it was a great achievement.

6 Ching Chang's caravan of men and beasts set out in the twilight of early morning. The faded moon was hanging in mid-sky and several isolated stars were still blinking. The party marched along a narrow footpath between rice fields on one side and cornfields on the other. The oxen led the way. They slouched along with slow, clumsy steps; the large bronze bells that tinkled dully from their necks could be heard half a mile away in the quiet morning. The two coolies walked behind the oxen. After them came the pigs. They grunted unceasingly, their noses pointed to the ground, utterly unmindful of what went on around them. Lucky, led by Sung with a fiber cord, trotted quietly after the pigs.

They met few people, and those they encountered were mostly the neighboring farmers. No one seemed to pay any attention to Lucky or even to notice him, so Sung untied the rope around the dog's neck and turned him loose. Lucky was exalted

with the freedom which he had lost for so long. He ran back and forth playfully along the column of pigs, but they ignored him completely. Now and then he would chase a frog or try to catch a grass-hopper but these usually jumped into the water or a thicket of rice. Sometimes a grasshopper would land right on the dog's forehead, and Lucky would shake his head vigorously to get rid of it.

A gentle breeze arose. The heads of the rice started to swing in a slow, graceful manner. Sung took a deep breath of the refreshing air.

Just then, a prolonged "*O ho ho . . .*" came from the coolies ahead. It was a warning signal. Ching Chang raised his head above the golden ears of rice, a hand over his brows to shade off the rising sun. "Men in uniforms!" he said urgently. "Hide the dog!"

Sung quickly caught Lucky, pushed him down into the paddy field, and jumped into it himself.

"No, that won't do," Ching Chang cried. "They

40

could trace you by the muddied water."

Sung pulled himself and Lucky out of the mud, wiped his feet on the sod, and ran into a cornfield on the other side of the road. At a distance of about fifty paces they stopped and squatted down among the cornstalks. Lucky tilted his head and gaped at Sung as if asking, "What's the matter? What are you doing?"

Sung did not heed him; he was busy listening to the approaching voices.

Suddenly Lucky gave a sharp bark and leaped to his feet. A snake was wriggling past a few feet away. Sung seized the dog and scolded, "Sit down and be quiet!"

Lucky sat down, but followed the snake with his eyes and licked his lips eagerly, as though he had a good appetite for it, until it disappeared in the weeds.

"I thought I heard a dog bark." A loud, distinct voice came from the road. Sung held his breath.

41

"Your fancy. How can there be a dog?" another voice responded.

"I'm sure I heard a dog."

Moments later, there was a gunshot. A bullet whistled through a row of corn and left a shower of broken blades in its wake. Sung dropped to his belly and pushed Lucky flat on the ground. The little dog remained quiet and fear was evident in his eyes.

"You are wasting your bullets, comrade," a loud voice exclaimed, and the statement was followed by a guffaw.

Sung crawled farther from the path of the bullet, dragging Lucky behind him and taking care not to disturb the cornstalks. He lay down again, listening and watching. As the men's voices grew fainter, Sung started to breathe again, and he became aware how violently his heart had been beating.

Finally a long *"Hou la . . ."* was heard from the distance. It was an all-clear signal from Ching Chang. Sung stood up, wiped the earth and weeds from his clothes, and ran with Lucky to join the caravan.

"Just a few militiamen," Ching Chang said contemptuously. "They wouldn't have dared touch the dog if I told them who I am and why I need the dog."

Presently they came to a stony hillside, where a large crowd of men and women were digging with spades, hoes, and shovels, and three or four women were sitting on the ground and crying in chanting, mournful voices and frequently wiping their eyes. Lucky stopped, looked, and barked softly.

"Quiet," Sung cried.

Lucky suddenly darted off and ran to a pile of something on the outskirts of the crowd. Sung dashed after him and discovered that it was a pile of human bones, with limbs and skulls complete, that Lucky was after. Some paces from the mound was another pile of decayed wood that obviously had been coffins. Sung turned his head, dismayed, and quickly pulled the dog away.

"Do you know what these people are doing?" he asked Ching Chang.

"Of course, digging up the graves," Ching Chang replied. "I've seen it many times."

"Why are they doing that?"

"To make room for crops, and the bones are to be

used for fertilizer."

"But how can the poor, stony ground used for cemeteries grow anything?"

"I've seen them digging worse land. It's a waste of time, but they do it, because they have to obey orders from above."

"Why are the women crying?"

"Because their dear ones, maybe husbands or children, are buried here. It's old wounds reopened, and old memories remembered," Ching Chang said carelessly. Then he turned to the other side of the hill and, pointing with his smoking pipe, changed the subject. "You see the embankment there and the thing that gleams? That's the iron road. We will follow it all the way to Canton. Even a blind man could make it."

"Is *that* the iron road?" Sung asked, staring at the long gleaming rails resting on wooden planks. "I thought the iron road was paved with iron plates."

"I had thought so too," Ching Chang said, "until I saw it."

There was a considerable amount of foot and bicycle traffic along the sides of the railroad track. This worried Sung. He looked around. The track was straight as far as his eyes could reach, and the topography was flat and mostly bare on either side, so it would be difficult to run for shelter. As he trudged along under the sun, which was growing hotter and hotter, he was overwhelmed with anxiety. However, after a while, he began to realize that the passers-by were preoccupied with themselves and too bothered by the hot sun to care about anything else. Most of them traveled in quick strides, their heads half hidden by umbrellas or wide-rimmed, woven-straw hats.

Sung also noticed that their own caravan almost had a monopoly of one side of the track. As the pedestrians approached the heavily loaded oxen and the scampering, stinking pigs, they invariably crossed the track to the other side to avoid them. Few so much as cast a glance at the pigs, let alone singled out the little black dog among them. Many held their noses and spat and turned their heads away as they passed. Men in uniforms were few, and most of them rode on bicycles and went by swiftly.

At midday they arrived at a fairly wide river that was spanned by an iron bridge. The water was rather clear and several men were bathing in it. Groves of vigorous bamboos decorated the bank on either side and they were irresistibly inviting to the travelers. The coolies drove the oxen into the shade, removed their loads, and led them to the water. The oxen sucked the water like pumps, while the pigs scattered into the bamboo groves and collapsed.

Water was fetched from the river, and it was mixed with rice bran and soybean leaves taken from the loads carried by the oxen. At once the pigs became alive and rushed to the feeding pans and devoured everything greedily and noisily.

When the animals had been fed, the men sat down in a circle in the shade and began to feed themselves and smoke. Sung shared his food with

Lucky. Then they all stretched out flat on their backs, Lucky huddling between Ching Chang and Sung with one end of his leash tied to Sung's ankle. Everybody became quiet. They rested until the sun had gone far down in the west and the heat had abated before resuming their journey.

The coolies loaded the oxen while Ching Chang and Sung aroused the pigs with the bamboo whips and drove them toward the railroad. But when they reached the head of the bridge, neither the oxen nor the pigs would move forward. The coolies tried to pull the oxen by the rope that passed through their nostrils while whipping them from behind, but it was impossible to make the stubborn animals set their feet on the bridge. They were afraid of the water down below, which they could see clearly through the sleepers.

Finally, the coolies drove the oxen down the bank and tried to wade across the river. The water was not too deep for the oxen, but it was deep enough to soak the rice bran and the dry soybean leaves they carried. The burdens became so heavy that the poor beasts collapsed in the middle of the river. The coolies had to dip the wet contents from the bags and baskets and carry it to the shore lump by lump, until the oxen were able to move.

Meanwhile, Ching Chang and Sung were trying to urge the pigs to walk across the bridge, but they only succeeded in driving them to scatter in different directions. Ching Chang worked so hard his shirt became thoroughly soaked with sweat, so he took it off, sat down on the ground, lit his pipe, and tried to figure out a way to solve the problem.

"Too bad there is no sampan around, or that these brutes cannot swim," he complained. He twirled the coarse hair of his wart so nervously that Sung feared he was going to pull it off.

"Why don't we carry them over?" Sung suggested.

"Carry them over!" Ching Chang cried. "Who's going to carry them over? They are so many and so heavy." He continued to twirl his big hair with his pudgy fingers while he puffed nervously at his pipe. Then suddenly he sprang to his feet, tucked the smoking pipe in the belt of his trousers, and said, "We must beat them hard. Pigs are pigs."

Picking up a split bamboo cane, he raised it high into the air and thrashed the pigs all around. The poor beasts were so frightened they stampeded, and three of them plunged headlong and dropped through the beams of the bridge into the river. The bathers and onlookers below laughed and shouted and rushed to the rescue, splashing up curtains of water in their efforts. After much struggling, all three pigs were caught and brought ashore.

"Bring them here, bring the pigs to me," Ching Chang shouted importantly at the rescuers.

But the men were running away from him, while Ching Chang continued to shout, "You men, bring the pigs to me, I'll reward you."

They only ran faster and disappeared behind the bamboo groves.

"What do they want to do with the pigs?" Ching

Chang asked Sung helplessly.

"They want to carry them away." Sung said the obvious thing.

"Is there anything we can do about it?"

"Chase them."

Ching Chang threw up his hands in despair and cursed. "The thieves! Let them eat the pork and get dysentery and cholera." He turned to Sung. "We've got to carry them over, as you said. But how are we going to manage it? We are only two, but we must have one at each end of the bridge to keep watch and another to do the carrying."

"Why don't you ask a coolie to help?" Sung suggested.

"Ah, you are smart! How stupid *I* am! Coolie . . . coolie . . . ," he shouted, "go over there to the bridgehead and wait for me."

Ching Chang began to carry the pigs over the bridge, two at a time. On the last trip, he was followed by Sung, who carried Lucky. When they arrived at the farther end, Ching Chang threw the pigs on the ground heavily, and as they shrieked and scurried away, he groaned, "My God, how tired I am! I must thank the thieves for saving me more trips with the pigs they stole."

After a brief rest, they continued their journey and arrived at a village called Fushing Market Place when the sun was just a carrying pole above the horizon. No inn would accommodate them, so they took shelter in an empty, partly ruined temple for the night.

7 Both men and beasts were tired after the day's travel, especially from the troubles at the railroad bridge. Ching Chang and Sung and the coolies slept late the following morning and were finally aroused by loud noises from the street. It was a market day at Fushing Market Place. Farmers and farm women had been pouring in from the surrounding areas since dawn. They brought chickens and ducks with their feet tied with straws; pigs with ropes around their necks; grains, beans, other vegetables, and fuel branches in sacks, baskets, and bundles. Quack doctors, food vendors, and peddlers of sundry goods had spread out their wares or pitched their tents in the street and the courtyards of temples and monasteries. They howled over their commodities and haggled endlessly with the customers.

Sung woke first. He blinked at the daylight and was astonished. "Get up and be going!" he shouted out at the others. "It's almost noontime."

It took a long while and some vigorous pushing and shaking from Sung to make Ching Chang and the coolies wake and get up. They quickly fed the oxen and the pigs. Then with pipes between their lips, the coolies fastened the loads on the oxen, and the caravan was on its way in the order of the previous day—the oxen first, followed by the coolies, then the pigs, and finally Ching Chang, Sung, and Lucky.

The street was narrow, crowded, and noisy, so the coolies had to keep shouting at the tops of their voices: "Make way! Make way for the oxen! They'll knock you down and tramp on you."

But the crowd appeared to be deaf until the oxen actually bumped against their backs or trod on their feet. Then they would turn fierce faces and swear vehemently, demanding, "Don't you have eyes?"

The pigs had even greater trouble in boring through the human masses. No matter how loudly Ching Chang and Sung yelled and howled, the way remained tightly blocked to them. Finally, Ching Chang lost patience, and he gave several pigs a heavy thrashing with his split bamboo. Two pigs plunged into a snack stand that was supported by a slim tripod and knocked it over, shattering the bowls and dishes and spilling the rice-flour balls and the rice wine.

The standkeeper was a small, bony, but very energetic woman with a terrible voice. She instantly exploded, acting as if she had gone mad. She screamed, shook her fists, pulled her hair, and stamped her feet. She kicked the pigs left and right, then picked up the broken pieces of china and pelted the pigs with them.

The pigs stampeded. They ran into earthenware crocks and baskets of eggs and smashed them. They trod on chickens and ducks and sent them on the wing. They also knocked down drug stalls and eating stands. There was a riot of the most boisterous kind. One would think that a hundred wolves had invaded the market place and were devouring the marketers. Everybody was shouting, "*Dah . . . dah . . . dah!* Beat . . . beat . . . beat!" Many picked up poles and sticks, broken dishes and stones, and hit the pigs with them. Ching Chang and Sung begged and exhorted the crowd to stop the free-for-all, but they were ignored.

At last when the mob had had enough of the fun and quieted down, Ching Chang and Sung collected the scattered pigs in a corner of the terrace in front of the monastery, counted them, and found two missing.

"You stay here and keep watch," Ching Chang said to Sung, wiping his forehead with a sweaty hand, "while I go to search for them."

As he turned to go, Ching Chang found his way blocked by an angry mob. The men yelled and shook their fists at him. One voice was especially loud and clear: "You stinky swine drover, come and see what your pigs have done. . . . You are not going to get away with it . . ." They seized Ching Chang like a pack of fierce dogs seizing a deer and dragged him by his shirt, by his pants, by his arms, even by his ears and hair to a teahouse, the usual place for business transactions and settlement of disputes.

Sung, assisted by a coolie and the dog, tried to keep the pigs from scattering. It was no easy task after all the violent commotion and amidst the hustle and bustle of the market, but finally the pigs were quieted. Sung sat down on the stone steps in front of the gate of the monastery. Lucky flung himself down beside him, panting. Suddenly, seemingly out of nowhere, a dwarfish militiaman, a rifle on his shoulder and a haughty expression on his face, appeared and demanded, "How is it you have a dog?"

"He has always belonged to me," replied Sung, trying not to show his terror.

"No one may keep a dog," the militiaman pronounced in the tone and manner of a judge handing down a sentence. "He has to be killed." And he reached out to grab the leash.

Sung threw his arms around Lucky and protested, "No, you can't kill him, you can't. Let me explain it to you, please. This dog has an official duty, he is . . . he is . . . an official."

"An official! A dog is an official?" The little militiaman laughed uproariously. Then his face fell back to its stern lines and he said, "Official or no official, he has to be killed and eaten." And he tried to unlock Sung's arms from the dog.

Lucky bared his teeth and growled. The militiaman drew back.

"Be quiet," Sung commanded. "He really has an

official duty," the boy said to the militiaman, making an effort to sound important. "He helps to manage these pigs, which are government property."

The militiaman considered this a moment and said, "Show me the proof."

"My friend has the papers. He'll be back soon."

The militiaman thought for another moment or two, then shook his head incredulously and declared in a determined manner, "A dog is a dog. All dogs must be killed. It's Chairman Mao's order." He took the gun from his shoulder and, loading it, went on, "I am going to shoot him right here and now."

"No, no! Help, help!" Sung shouted, and threw himself over Lucky to protect him. A moment later, he heard Ching Chang's roaring voice. "Stop it! What are you trying to do to the boy?"

When Sung raised his head, Ching Chang had clutched the thin shoulders of the little militiaman with his large hands and was shaking him and demanding, "How dare you bully this boy?"

The militiaman struggled to tear himself loose but couldn't, and he fumed, "Who are you? How dare you interfere with my official duty? I want to kill that dog. Take your hands off me!"

Ching Chang let him go and said, "You will not. You cannot! He is my dog."

"All dogs must be killed."

"Not this one. He has an official duty."

"Where is the proof? Show me the proof!"

Ching Chang produced his official paper from his shirt pocket in a deliberately slow manner, unfolded it, and held it out to the militiaman, saying calmly, "Read it! Look at the official red seal."

The militiaman stared at the paper for a few moments, then slung his gun over his shoulder and sauntered away.

Sung heaved a deep sigh, wiped the beads of moisture from his forehead, and said, "How fortunate you returned just in time. If you had been a minute later, he would have killed Lucky, and perhaps me, also."

"Ah, my boy, you can rest at ease," Ching Chang, obviously pleased with himself, assured Sung. "I can guarantee your safety, and Lucky's safety, all the way to Canton. I did not realize how useful this piece of paper could be until I tried it out." Then he gave a bellow of laughter and went on, "You know, this little idiot of a militiaman is an illiterate. I held the paper upside down to him and he did not know it. He only saw the red seal, and that was enough to scare him away." Ching Chang gave another loud, ringing laugh and slapped his thigh.

"Have you found the pigs?" Sung asked.

"I found them all right, but I had to pay for the damages. I had no money to pay, so I paid with the pigs. They insisted that I had to settle with ten or more pigs. We argued and haggled; finally I produced my official paper and said to them that if they tried to extort money from me or detain me so that the pigs got sick, I'd report to the authorities and have them severely punished. So they gave in and accepted the two pigs for compensation."

8 The third morning Ching Chang's caravan again set out before dawn, following the railroad track as before. Everything went well except the temperature, which rose even higher than on the previous day. By noon it had become unbearably hot, so men and beasts were grateful to arrive at a cool spot.

There was a tunnel cut through a rocky hill, and before the opening was a large area of level ground, with several camphor trees that afforded inviting shade. Cool, damp air floated out of the tunnel, almost cool enough to make one shiver. It was very quiet and secluded there, almost serene. The only people about were three half-naked and dirty-faced urchins who were squatting on the ground and playing some sort of game with pebbles.

Ching Chang decided to take a long rest here, so he ordered the coolies to drive the oxen and the pigs to the shaded places and take the loads from the oxen. Sung unleashed Lucky, who at once went running and jumping about joyfully.

"A dog! Look at the dog!" one urchin cried out in a surprised voice as if he had seen a wild deer in a city street. He was a thickly pockmarked youngster of about thirteen or fourteen who had not had a haircut for a long time. "Is that your dog?" he asked Sung. "Why hasn't he been killed?"

"Why should he have been killed?" Sung snapped.

"What is his name?" a second boy asked.

Sung told him.

"Lucky? Lucky, Lucky," all three boys shouted, and beckoned with their dirty hands. Lucky only looked at them and refused to budge.

"I wish I had a bone," said the pockmarked boy.

"I have some popcorn," the second boy said. He went to a tattered shirt that hung on a tree, groped in the pocket, and scattered a handful of popped corn before him. "Come on, Lucky," he called, "Don't be bashful."

Lucky looked at the boy and the corn alternately, but remained where he was.

"He's afraid," said the pockmarked boy. "Let's move back a little."

The boys stepped away from the scattered popcorn, whereupon Lucky moved forward, sniffed at the corn, and began to pick it up. Then the boys gathered around him and admired him, stroking him on the back and the head.

"Boys," Ching Chang asked the urchins, "how

long is the tunnel?"

"Maybe one *li*," one replied.

"I think it's about two," from another.

"Maybe three," from the third.

Ching Chang laughed. "Can it be more than three or less than one *li*?"

"Who can say?" the pockmarked boy replied.

"Nuts!" Ching Chang said. "Is there any spring water nearby?"

"Yes, and it's very good," the boys answered in unison. The pockmarked boy added, "We can fetch you as much as you can drink for ten coppers."

"Including the oxen?" Ching Chang said.

"No, that would be fifty."

"All right," Ching Chang agreed. "Here is a pail."

They went away, all three of them, and returned with a pailful of clear water. It was just enough for the men. The boys went again and returned with a second pail of water. One ox sucked it into his stomach in one draft. And it was apparent that he wanted more. The boys made a third trip. Then they began to complain.

"An agreement is an agreement," Ching Chang said to them. "I will not pay you any money until the oxen have drunk all they want." He was tickled at his good bargain. The boys kept making trips until the oxen stopped drinking. Then Ching Chang paid the boys a dollar, which made them happier than the noisy magpies on the tops of the camphor trees.

Both men and beasts were invigorated by the

fresh spring water, and the prospect of walking through the cool tunnel was so tempting that they resumed the journey sooner than they had intended. When they had driven the oxen and the pigs into the tunnel, Ching Chang declared, "I don't mind if it is fifty *li* long, it's so pleasant inside." He was in such a joyous spirit that he started to whistle and sing in an absurdly high-pitched falsetto like a female singer.

"Long live Lucky!" Sung shouted out of sheer joy and for the fun of creating an echo.

The oxen had gone far ahead, but the resonant sound of their bells seemed very near. Even the pigs seemed to feel the effect of the refreshing air, for they trotted quietly in an orderly column. Lucky pranced gaily along and barked playfully.

Ching Chang estimated they had gone about two-thirds of the way through the tunnel when he suddenly stopped and said to Sung, "Do you hear something from the rails?"

"Yes, I was wondering," Sung replied. "I think the rails are giving off a faint sound."

"Maybe a train is coming," Ching Chang said with alarm. "Why didn't we ask before we entered? *Ho shu! Ho shu!*" he shouted to the pigs to make them go faster. "We saw only one train all day yesterday."

The sound from the rails grew louder, and they started to tremble.

"*Ho shu! Ho shu!*" Ching Chang shouted again and whipped the pigs. "I'm afraid it's too late to get out. Keep them away from the track, Sung."

Just as they succeeded in driving the pigs from the track to the sides of the tunnel, the train gave a terrifying whistle outside the opening. The sound had hardly died away before the train thundered inside and filled the tunnel with hot air, smoke, and confusion. The frightened pigs shrieked and scuttled helter-skelter. Ching Chang and Sung plugged their ears with both hands and closed their eyes. The commotion lasted for only about a minute, but Sung found it a frightful experience. When he opened his eyes, he saw blood and the mangled carcasses of dead pigs strewn all over.

"Lucky! Lucky!" he shouted in terror. He ran back and forth and kept shouting, "Lucky! Lucky! Where are you?"

"Lucky, Lucky, damn it!" Ching Chang swore vehemently. "It's not lucky, it's most unlucky. Look how many pigs have been killed!"

They collected the dead pigs and piled the bodies against the wall of the tunnel. With a thumping heart, Sung inspected them for the remains of Lucky. He was overjoyed when he failed to find him. Lucky must be alive and might come back to him presently, wagging his tail and body to tell how scared he had been and how happy he was to be with him again.

"Lucky, Lucky," Sung called toward one end of the tunnel, then the other. But Lucky did not appear.

"Why don't you look outside?" Ching Chang suggested.

Sung ran forward out of the tunnel, looked all around and shouted, but there was no Lucky. An elderly woman kept a food stall beside the opening, and several travelers were standing around eating bowls of noodles and *hsi fan,* a thin, watery rice called congee by Westerners. Sung asked the woman if she had seen a black dog come out of the tunnel a while ago.

"No," she replied, while the travelers agreed. One of them said, "We haven't seen any dog for a long time, black or white."

Sung returned to the tunnel and searched all the way back to the other end. There was no trace of Lucky. Sung explored every corner of the terrace where they had rested, and with hands cupped before his mouth, shouted, "Luck . . . y, Luck . . . y." He was answered only by the echoes from the dark rocks around him. He wished there was someone about who could give him some clue, but not a soul was in sight. The three urchins who had been playing there a while ago had all gone, probably to spend their dollar. Sung's heart sank.

He trudged back through the tunnel with a bent head, no longer searching. Ching Chang had moved the pig carcasses outside and was standing beside the pile. He turned around and asked, "Did you find him?"

"No," Sung replied sadly, almost in tears.

"Maybe he has run ahead of us and is with the coolies," Ching Chang suggested hopefully.

"Yes," Sung cried excitedly. "He must have!" At once he started to run.

"Wait a minute," Ching Chang shouted to him. "You see the village down there on the left of the railroad behind those trees? That's Tai-ping Market Place. We'll stop there tonight. I know the innkeeper and his wife. Tell them that I'm coming and we will have a big feast with all this pork. Even Lucky will have an all-meat dinner, not just bones. Now run along, and cheer up."

Sung dashed to Tai-ping village as fast as his tired legs could carry him. From a distance he saw the oxen resting at the end of the street, chewing their cuds; then he noticed the coolies sitting at a table outside the door of a teahouse, puffing at their pipes. As he left the railroad and started along the footpath, he shouted to them, "Is Lucky with you?"

"Lucky with us? Why, of course not," one coolie replied, while the other merely shook his head with the pipe in his mouth. "He was with you all the time, wasn't he?"

Sung's heart sank again, and it sank so heavily that his flushed face turned pale abruptly.

The other coolie pulled his pipe out of his lips and asked, "What is the matter? Is he lost?"

When Sung told them of the accident, the coolies began making guesses as to the fate of Lucky, and they concluded that he must have been caught in the wheels of the train and carried away.

"No, that can't be!" Sung cried. He turned back and ran in the direction from which he had come. At the junction of the footpath with the railroad, he encountered Ching Chang, followed by several coolies he had hired to carry the pork.

"Where are you going?" Ching Chang demanded.

"Lucky is not there," replied Sung.

"You mean you are going back to the tunnel to search again?"

"Yes."

Ching Chang clutched Sung's slender arm and turned him back. "Why waste more time?" he said severely. "He must have been caught in the wheels of the train and carried away." He forced Sung in the direction of the village. When they reached the teahouse, Ching Chang ordered the coolies to transfer the load of meat to the oxen, and the caravan proceeded to the inn. Sung plodded along behind like a sleepwalker.

9 It was indeed a big dinner that the innkeeper and his wife prepared for Ching Chang's party, even though there was no fish, no chicken, and neither wild game from the mountains nor rarities from the sea—things considered essential for a true feast in China. But the pig has many different parts and organs with as many different textures and tastes. The kidneys, liver, stomach, brains, ears, feet, snout—each made a separate dish. And there are many ways of cooking the pork. The innkeeper and his wife were highly proficient in this art. They boiled some in water first, then cut it in thin slices and cooked it in a pan of soy sauce, garlic, ginger, and hot peppers. Some pork was chopped into slender strips as fine as silk threads and cooked with bean sprouts, bamboo shoots, and mushrooms; some was cut into lumps, then mixed with beaten egg and wheat flour and fried in deep oil; some was fried in deep oil with the skin on, then sliced, seasoned, and

63

steamed. The odors and the sounds of chopping and frying ordinarily would have attracted all the dogs of the village to the inn, but there wasn't a single dog in sight.

The large table was piled with heaping bowls and dishes. The mere sight of it could make one's mouth water. The coolies swallowed their saliva visibly as they sat down at the table. Everyone ate ravenously and with concentrated attention. Perspiration glistened on brows; oil circled mouths and dripped from chins. Ching Chang challenged the innkeeper to play the finger game.

The two began to fling out their hands, shouting out their guesses at the total number of fingers showing. The loser had to down a glass of wine. As Ching Chang lost most of the games, he had to drink most of the wine as a penalty. He grew more and more excited, and as his face turned redder, the wart on his chin seemed to grow blacker. He began to brag about the sights and excitements of Canton, which he had visited once before. Suddenly he turned to Sung as though he had not noticed his presence until that moment and demanded, "Why are you so quiet, my boy?"

Sung was brooding over the loss of Lucky. He could not understand how Lucky had disappeared, and he stubbornly refused to accept the plausible explanation that the dog had been caught in the wheels of the train and carried away. "He must have fled somewhere and is still alive. I must search for him," he kept telling himself again and again. He forced a smile without answering Ching Chang's question.

"Are you still mourning over the dog?" Ching Chang insisted, around a great mouthful. "Why don't you forget him?"

"I'll go home tomorrow," Sung said gloomily.

"Why?"

"Maybe Lucky is heading for home, and I can find him on the way."

Ching Chang swallowed the pork in his mouth, wiped his chin with the back of his hand, and then said more articulately, "If he had tried to go home, he must have been captured and killed already. Why don't you forget him? It may be a good thing that he has disappeared. You'd have to give him away, anyhow."

"There's no need for me to go to Canton now."

"Don't you want to see a big city? Don't you want to see big stores and buildings taller than the tallest tree you've ever seen?"

Sung only shook his head.

When the feast was only half through, Sung got up to leave.

"Where are you going?" Ching Chang asked.

"I want to put on more clothes," Sung replied without looking back.

"You mean you are cold? That's strange. I'm hot. Bring back my fan."

Sung shuffled to the bedroom, put on an extra shirt, and returned with a large palm-leaf fan for Ching Chang.

"Why don't you drink some *kaoliang* wine? It will warm you up," Ching Chang said, and poured a tiny cupful of the sorghum liquor for Sung. The boy gulped it down.

"You feel better?" Ching Chang asked.

Sung replied with an uncertain nod. After a few minutes it became evident that the liquor had not done him any good. He began to shiver, and his teeth clicked. So he returned to the bedroom, lay down, and pulled the quilt over him.

Meanwhile, the innkeeper's wife was telling the feasters at the table in a cautious whisper, "I'm afraid he's sick, he looks so pale."

"I'm afraid it's malaria," her husband blurted out.

"Hush! Hush! Don't mention it," the woman said reproachfully. "When that thing attacks, one should never mention it."

"That's superstition," Ching Chang said with a superior air. He put down his chopsticks, wiped his lips and chin with both hands, and staggered to the bedroom. Sung was groaning and the bed was shaking.

"I see you are cold. Do you want more quilts?" Ching Chang asked.

"Yes, please." Sung's voice trembled.

Ching Chang picked up the quilt from his own bed and spread it over Sung. He returned to the dining table and asked the innkeeper and his wife whether they could recommend a doctor.

66

"We have only an herb shop," the innkeeper replied, "and it is now closed."

"Why a doctor?" his wife asked in a loud voice. "No doctor or drug can cure this disease. The only way to get cured is to run away from it."

"How do you do that?" Ching Chang asked.

"You just run away to some place before the attack begins so that the disease cannot find you."

"That's superstition," Ching Chang said again.

"Superstition!" the woman exclaimed, the fleshy rolls on her body rippling. "What do you mean by superstition? I know many, many malaria victims are cured that way." She went on to cite example after example of how so and so had been cured by simply running away.

Ching Chang cut her short by resolutely shaking his head, and he warned, "Don't you try to cure that boy by that method."

The innkeeper's wife made a wry face, threw up her fat hands, and fell silent.

Sung continued to shake and complain of cold until midnight. Then he kicked off all the covers and complained of being hot. He groaned even more during this period than he had during the chilly period. He ground his teeth and talked in his sleep. By the end of the night he quieted, then went soundly to sleep.

10 When Sung got up in midmorning, Ching Chang and his party had already left. Ching Chang had decided that Sung could not make the trip to Canton, so he left some money with the innkeeper and his wife and asked them to take good care of the boy until he returned.

"Don't try to cure him by escaping," he admonished the innkeeper's wife once more. The latter turned her head away and made a face.

In the afternoon, when Sung thought that he had recovered, he went to the kitchen and told the innkeeper's wife that he wanted to go to the railway tunnel to look for the dog.

"Do you feel strong enough to make the trip?" she asked, putting a motherly hand on his temple to feel his temperature. She was secretly pleased that without being told to, Sung was unwittingly following her remedy. She knew that the malaria would attack again, probably later in the evening, but believed in spite of Ching Chang's scorn that Sung could escape it by hiding in some other place. So she said, "All right, if you want to go, I'll pack some food for you to take along, for you may be late coming home."

When Sung arrived at the tunnel, the woman vendor was encouraging the mud stove with a large fan of woven bamboo splinters and sending up clouds of dark smoke. Sung walked up behind her and greeted her with, "Good afternoon, old grandmother. May I help you?"

The woman gave a start, turned her smudged face to him, and replied, "Ah! It's the boy who lost his dog here yesterday. Have you found him?"

"No. Do you have any news for me?"

"I wish I had."

Sung took the fan from the woman and attacked the fire vigorously. In a minute or two the stove was in full blaze and the smoke had disappeared. Sung was too anxious to look for Lucky to do anything else for long, so he laid the fan on a bench and entered the tunnel. He searched all the way through, straining his eyes, hoping that he might find Lucky huddled somewhere against the wall. At the same time, he was fearful that he might discover the dog's corpse, or parts of it. When he reached the other end of the tunnel without detecting any trace of Lucky, he was both disappointed and relieved—disappointed because he had not found him; relieved because he had found no evidence of his death. Lucky must still be alive!

By now, Sung was feeling weak and tired. He lay down on a stone bench under a camphor tree outside the tunnel. The bench was hard but comfortably warm, not hot. Whenever a traveler came by, Sung would ask him if he had seen a black dog with white paws. No one had.

Sung stayed until the sun went down and the air cooled off. When he began to feel chilly, he started back to the inn. The chill grew rapidly in intensity. It was not the weather but a renewed attack of the malaria. The boy groaned and shivered, like a beggar in deep winter, as he trudged along.

This second attack was more severe than the first. Then there came the third and the fourth. He had to stay in bed most of the time. Each day he became thinner, paler, and weaker. He groaned and ground his teeth, and dreamed of home every night. The innkeeper's wife blamed him for lacking faith in her prescription.

One afternoon while Sung was lying in bed after an attack of the malaria, he felt a large rough hand on his forehead and heard a familiar voice. "How do you feel?"

Sung opened his eyes and saw one of the coolies.

"Ah, you are back!" he cried. "Where is Ching Chang?"

"He's still in Canton."

"Why did he stay?"

"He has to teach the comrades how to feed pigs."

"Don't the farmers there know how to feed pigs?"

"Of course they do, but the comrades wouldn't

trust them, because they had been cheated by them. Once the farmers advised them to feed the pigs with useless things such as rice husks, peanut shells, corn-cobs, and fallen leaves so that grain could be saved for human consumption. The comrades took the advice seriously and issued orders to the villagers of Kwangtung Province to adopt the new method. They did. It resulted in the death and sickness of many thousands of pigs. So they don't trust the farmers any more." The coolie burst into laughter as he finished. Then he groped in a sack, produced a small package, and went on, "I have brought you some money and foreign medicine. They say the medicine is very effective for your disease. It's called quinine. Do you want to take some right now?"

Sung nodded and the coolie went for some water.

"Put the pill in your mouth, don't chew, but swallow it with the water."

Sung swallowed all the water, but the pill remained in his mouth. He had never taken any pills before, only Chinese herb soups. Finally he crushed the pill with his teeth, then choked it down.

The innkeeper's wife had no confidence in the foreign pills, but she did not forbid Sung to take them. When after a few days Sung was actually cured, she was more perplexed than pleased. She told everybody that the evil spirit of the disease had had enough of the boy so it had left him.

Before Sung had completely recovered his strength, he resumed his search for Lucky. He was confident that his dog was still alive somewhere and that if he persisted he would find him. His faith was strengthened when, at the eating stall outside the railway tunnel, he ran into several travelers who were talking about a street circus with a performing monkey and a dog. The mention of a dog immediately caught Sung's attention, so he went up to the travelers and asked, "What kind of dog is it?"

"It's a little black dog, and very cute," replied one of the travelers.

"Are his paws white?"

"Who pays attention to the paws?"

"Does he have a name?"

"The circus man called him Lucky."

"That's my dog!" Sung cried out, so loudly that the traveler started.

"He lost a dog here a few days ago," the food vendor explained. "He's been back to look and inquire many times. It's a little black dog."

"I see!" said the traveler. "But many, many dogs are black."

"But if his name is Lucky?" Sung argued.

"That is a very common name for a dog," the traveler pointed out.

"Not many dogs are black *and* named Lucky."

"But how could the man know your dog's name?" the traveler objected.

Sung stopped arguing and asked instead where the traveler had seen the monkey circus.

"Oh, I think it was at Sah-ping Market Place."

"That's about thirty miles from here," the food vendor put in.

"But it drifts from place to place like leaves in a hurricane," said the traveler.

Sung was at first both excited and hopeful over the news. However, he calmed down as he walked back to Tai-ping village, and doubts began to dawn in his mind. Indeed, as the traveler had said, a great many dogs were black and a great many dogs were named Lucky. Moreover, how could Lucky have gotten into a monkey circus? How could he have learned to perform in such a short time? At these thoughts, Sung became uncertain and depressed.

However, a little later hope arose in him again. There weren't many dogs left nowadays, he thought, black or white, Lucky or of any other name. He had not seen a single dog throughout the journey. So it must be his dog, it must be Lucky. He would search for him all over the area, even though the monkey circus drifted like the leaves in a hurricane, as the traveler had said.

First of all, Sung decided, he would make a trip to Sah-ping village. If the circus was not there, he could find out where it had gone. Sung decided to go at his search methodically. He obtained from the innkeeper and his wife the names of the surrounding villages, the distances between them, and their market days. A crude map was drawn. He found out that on the way to Sah-ping village he had to pass several other villages. Possibly he would find the circus in one of them; then he wouldn't have to proceed to Sah-ping.

11 Sung set out on his search one morning before sunrise, with the money Ching Chang had sent him in a little cloth bag securely tied around his waist, and several muffins and some preserved vegetables wrapped in lotus leaves. The minute he set foot outside the village, the memory of the first morning he had left home returned to him vividly. For a while he felt lonely and even sad. But the prospect of recovering Lucky cheered him, and he walked on jauntily. He traveled at first over a country of gentle hills, densely dotted by farmhouses with black tile roofs and white-plastered walls. From each and every one of these smoke rose, and it lingered as if unwilling to disperse. Here and there farmers would emerge from creaking doors, carrying hoes, baskets, or wooden pails, their brown limbs gleaming in the horizontal rays of the sun. As the morning advanced, the voices of women and children were heard, loud and long, calling their men in the fields to come home for breakfast.

Sung had not felt hungry, but the breakfast calls aroused his appetite. He looked for some shaded place to eat, but there was none, and as he did not want to waste time anyway, he opened his food packages and ate while walking. The muffin and preserved vegetables were delicious, but he had to have some water. He looked for a well or pond, but there was none in sight. The paddy fields were nearly dry, and if there was any water in them, it was muddy.

Then Sung saw a man in a large straw hat carrying two pails of water slung over his shoulder on a pole. He was trotting briskly toward him from the opposite direction. Sung greeted him with, "Good day, uncle water carrier, may I have a little of your water to appease my thirst?"

"Certainly you may," the man said pleasantly, and put the pails down on the edge of the road. "It's good cool water from our stone-lined well. I see you are a traveler. Drink as much as your stomach can hold, for the day will be hot."

Sung put his mouth in the pail and sucked the water eagerly until his stomach could not take in any more. He thanked the carrier and went on. It was not hot, it was not cold, and his stomach was full. The boy was in excellent spirits, and walked with quick, jaunty strides. He looked up at the sky and around over the golden fields in the valley and breathed the fresh air. He itched to sing. By patterning after a popular folksong he remembered, he composed a song of his own and chanted,

75

A white cloud floats over my head,
A light breeze cools my face;
Oh, Lucky, I'll search you out
From market place to market place.

As he sang in a low, merry voice, he came upon a
wedding procession. Two teenagers walked first,
one carrying the national flag and the other a large
printed portrait of Chairman Mao Tse-tung. In
their wake were two other boys, each carrying a

gong and beating it with the knot of a rope made of rice straw. Then came the dowry—quilts, mosquito net, long pillows, red-painted wooden trunks, bedroom furniture, and a small radio painted red and carried in a rack by two men to display it. These were followed by several sedan chairs carrying the matchmaker, the representatives of the two families, the bridegroom, and the bride. All the sedans were plain ones, made of bamboo mats and borne by bamboo poles resting on the shoulders of two men, except for the bride's. Hers was bigger, painted and draped with embroidered silk, and carried by four men. The bride's sedan was preceded by a four-man orchestra consisting of two trumpets, a small drum, and a small gong. Sung wished to have a look at the bride, but the sedan was tightly sealed, with no crack for a peep.

"This is an old-fashioned wedding," Sung thought, "like those of the big landlords and rich merchants." But as there were no landlords and rich merchants any more, he knew these must be the families of the new officials.

Presently came another wedding procession, then several more. But none were as elaborate as the first. In one or two cases, even the bridegroom and the matchmaker traveled on foot; only the bride was carried, in an ordinary sedan. Sung could see her through the dilapidated curtain of coarse linen.

Whenever Sung encountered a wedding procession, he had to walk on the very edge of the narrow road to make way, and he became annoyed. Then the thought occurred to him that it must be a lucky day, and he cheered up. "It has got to be a lucky day," he thought. "Otherwise how can there be so many weddings?" If it was lucky for them, it was also lucky for him. He hadn't tried to choose a lucky day to make the trip, but there he was on a very lucky day. Lucky, his beloved Lucky, might be performing at the monkey circus in some nearby village at that very hour. Maybe he would find him soon, very soon, perhaps at the next village. He thought about how excited he would be when he found him, and how Lucky would run to him and jump in his arms, and cover his face with his tongue.

By now Sung knew for sure that he was approaching a large village and that it was a market day, because the traffic had grown so heavy. He grew more impatient and wished he could fly to the village. How slowly these ragged and emaciated farmers and farm women moved and how they blocked his way! They slouched along spiritlessly, loaded with the sacks or baskets they carried on their backs and shoulders, or dragging a pig or a goat that seemed unwilling to move at all.

At last Sung arrived at a big village, bigger than his home town. It had a long main street and a shorter back street. Today both streets were overflowing with marketers. Sung anxiously elbowed through the main street first, then the back. There was no monkey circus to be seen. Thirst and hunger had become unbearable, so the boy stopped at a teahouse to eat his remaining muffin. A small, hollow-cheeked waiter, whose apron was covered with so much grease that you could see your image in it, came with a cup and a soot-darkened bronze pot that had a foot-long spout. He poured hot liquid into the cup. Sung asked him whether there was a monkey circus at the village that day.

"No, not today," the waiter replied, "though we had one a few days ago."

"Not a few days ago, but a few *market* days ago," a customer at a nearby table corrected emphatically.

Sung did not try to ascertain whether it was just a few days ago or a few market days ago, because that would make only a small difference to him. He was happy to learn the news and he asked the customer, "Was there a little black dog with the circus?"

"Who cares for the dog? We're only interested in the monkey," the customer replied.

"That's right," said the waiter.

Never mind if they don't care for the dog, Sung thought. The important thing is that the monkey circus is around. If there is a monkey circus, there's sure to be a dog, because they always have one. Tomorrow the monkey circus is bound to be at Sah-ping village, because it is an important village and tomorrow is its market day.

Sung quickly gulped down his muffin and the tea, and at once resumed the journey. He wanted to arrive at Sah-ping that day so that he might find the monkey circus and Lucky early tomorrow.

12 Sung arrived in Sah-ping village with aching legs but a gay spirit. He washed his feet, had rice, fried soybeans, and pickled cucumber for supper, and immediately went to bed.

He shared a room with four coolies. He quickly went to sleep but before long was awakened by bedbugs. The coolies slept soundly and snored loudly. Sung both envied them and was annoyed by them. He wondered why the bugs did not bother them. Were they so accustomed to the biting that it no longer waked them, or had they developed something in their blood that repulsed the bugs? He kept asking himself this as he tossed about in the bed. The question, the snores, and the insects kept him awake or half-awake most of the night.

In spite of the sleeplessness, Sung brimmed with cheerfulness the following morning. He washed his face in a wooden basin with cold water and at once started to tour the streets. There were as yet only a few early risers around, mostly peddlers of chickens and ducks, vegetables, or firewood. The street became more and more crowded as the boy continued his journey from one end of the village to the other. He was on the alert all the time, expecting to bump into the circus man as he led the monkey and the dog to the market place or into the courtyard of a temple.

But more and more Sung became disappointed. He did not know how many trips he had made through the crowded street when he suddenly realized that the crowd had become thinner. The marketers were going home, but there was no monkey circus to be found.

Sung trudged back to the inn where he slumped on a bench, put his arms on the table, and laid his head on his arms. He was both exhausted and miserable.

"Have you found the monkey circus, young man?" he heard a voice ask from behind him.

Sung lifted his head and turned around. It was the bony, pale-looking proprietor of the inn, and he had a water pipe and a lighted paper spill in his hands. "No," the boy replied in a dejected voice.

The innkeeper sucked at the pipe, which made the water inside gurgle loudly as in a brook. Then he said, "If you want to see a monkey circus so badly, why don't you go to the *hsein* city (county seat), where every day is like a market day. If the circus is still around this area, that's the most likely place to find it. It's only about twenty miles from here."

Sung had been debating with himself whether he should search farther or return to Tai-ping village to wait for Ching Chang. The innkeeper's suggestion resolved his doubt. Yes, why not go to the city? Why leave that big stone unturned? He would have resumed his journey at once, but his aching feet and legs revolted. So he spent the night at the same inn. As on the previous night, he was bitten by bedbugs, but less severely. "They've had a good meal, so they aren't so hungry," Sung said to himself when he got up the following morning.

Being more fatigued and less impatient now, Sung started his journey later and traveled rather leisurely. He arrived at the *hsien* city at about the same time as the sun sank to earth. The county seat was surrounded by a high wall of large, darkened bricks, partly coated with moss and lichens. An arched tunnel through the wall formed a gate. There were two heavy doors studded with iron buttons, and a hitching stone which was sunk into the ground in the middle.

Sung slept at an inn just inside the gate and had the luxury of a small room all to himself. There were no coolies' snores and few bedbugs to annoy him, so he slept soundly throughout the night. There's no telling how long he would have stayed asleep in the morning but he was aroused by loud noises of gongs and drums, firecrackers and gunshots, and outbursts of cries and shouts. He sat up in alarm, rubbed his eyes, and pricked up his ears.

"What is it? Where am I?" he asked. When he

83

remembered where he was, he jumped out of bed and ran to the street to see what all the hubbub was about. Gangs of children and men and women were running about in excitement, shouting and laughing. Many carried poles and sticks, gongs, drums, pots, earthen or tin washbasins, and trumpets, and were waving, beating, or blowing them. Many of their faces were turned upward, so Sung looked up too. The sky was covered with dark clouds, but there seemed nothing unusual about it. Then he saw several men on the roofs of houses and wondered what they were doing up there.

Just then, a mass of dry weeds dropped in front of him. It was a bird's nest, with some old feathers stuck to it. He stepped forward to pick it up. As he did, he felt a warm, soft object fall into his collar, making his flesh creep. He dipped it out and looked into his hand. He held a baby sparrow, pinkish and featherless, and still alive! He hastily tossed it on the ground as if it were a biting snake.

Sung understood at once. "Is it the Annihilate-the-Sparrows campaign?" he asked an elderly woman who was standing beside him.

"What else do you think it is?" the woman retorted. "They want to kill all the sparrows because they steal our grains. You should go to help. Everybody must help; that's the magistrate's order."

"I must have my breakfast first," Sung said and quickly turned away. He returned to the inn, washed up, and ate a bowl of congee with preserved vegetables and beans. He was not interested in

hunting sparrows; he wanted to hunt for the monkey circus and find his dog. To his chagrin, when he returned to the street, he learned that all business was suspended for the day. The doors of stores were closed so that the inhabitants of the city could all engage in the Annihilate-the-Sparrows campaign.

The street presented the appearance of a strange sort of carnival, quite unlike an ordinary festival. There were people on every house top, removing the roof tiles to search for the nests of sparrows. Everybody was shouting or making noise with some utensil or instrument. Uniformed men fired guns and pistols, either to kill the sparrows or to scare them. Lighted firecrackers were pitched at the birds. The frightened sparrows had no place to perch. They flew back and forth and circled around, or tried to hide in some sheltered spot. But there was no safe place for them, because every place was sentineled. Some were hit by gunshots, others by poles. Many dropped dead because they had eaten poisoned bait; others from exhaustion. There were always children rushing to pick up the sparrows that fell to the ground, fighting and quarreling over them in loud, high-pitched voices. Many of the sparrows were still alive; their eyes were open and their chests heaved. Some children treated these birds with tenderness and tried to nurse them, but they soon died.

As Sung pushed and elbowed through the street, he encountered a cluster of uniformed men a few houses from the *hsien yamen,* the magistrate's house. One of these, a slightly built young man wearing a visored cap, a new blue tunic, and dark sunglasses (although the sun was not visible), and carrying a lacquered walking stick with a brass top, was speaking animatedly to the others, who carried pistols and guns. One of the men had a linen bag which apparently contained captured sparrows, because there were stirs and chirps from inside it.

"The magistrate!" Sung heard a low voice from behind him. He turned around and asked, "Which one?"

"The one who carries the cane and wears dark glasses."

Sung had never seen a magistrate before. He had a vague notion that a magistrate must be a big, fat man with a terrible voice which excited awe. But this one seemed to be an ordinary man in every respect, so the boy could hardly believe the bystander's words. He moved closer, not, of course, without some trepidation, and pricked up his ears. "We must exterminate all the sparrows before the day gets dark," Sung heard the slight young man say.

"Yes, magistrate," several voices replied in unison.

"I'll hold you responsible if I find a single sparrow tomorrow," the magistrate said, beating the stone pavement with his cane. For almost half a minute his attendants said nothing, and they looked frightened.

Then one of them said, "We'll do our best."

"We must kill *all* of them," the magistrate repeated.

"They may flee out of the city today and return tomorrow," another man said.

"They may not want to return to the city," said a third, "because they can fare just as well in the crop fields. But they could also do more damage to the farmers than in the cities. And it is more difficult to hunt them in the open country."

"Difficult?" the magistrate cried. "Did you say it's difficult to fight a small bird like the sparrow? Nonsense! Easy or difficult, all the sparrows in the whole country must be exterminated, the same as rats and cats and flies and dogs. It's Chairman Mao's order. Nothing is difficult if you have mastered Chairman Mao's teachings."

"Yes, magistrate," the several attendants said in one voice, and they bowed their heads and remained silent.

Sung backed away, satisfied that he had seen a magistrate, but also disillusioned that he looked even less impressive than his friend Ching Chang.

Now Sung began to roam the streets in order to get acquainted with them. The city was not only much bigger than any village he had visited but also more complicated. It had four main streets arranged in a cross and named East, South, West, and North, each leading to a gate named after the direction it faced. There were several lesser streets besides. Sung lost his way several times, but he found the *yamen*

and realized where he was.

By noon, the sparrow hunters had dispersed, the stores opened, and the streets resumed their normal activities. It was time for the monkey circus to start if it was in the city. Sung toured all the streets and visited all the temples and monasteries. He went through them again and again and looked and asked until the sun had set, but he found no trace or shadow of a monkey circus.

Disappointed and saddened, Sung wanted to cry. He would have cried if he had been alone, but there were people everywhere in the city. It was not such a long distance he had covered, but he felt as tired as if he had traveled a whole day on a country road.

To add to his misfortune, the innkeeper charged him an exorbitant price for the room and meals. The sum frightened him because he did not have it. He argued hotly with the man, but the latter wouldn't yield a penny. Finally Sung paid with all the money he had, and he had to show the innkeeper his empty pockets and allow him to search his body. The innkeeper still grumbled and fumed as if he had been outrageously cheated.

Now Sung's immediate problem was how to return to Tai-ping village without money or food.

13 Sung asked several men in the street whether there was a short cut to Tai-ping village. To his chagrin, none of them even knew of such a place. Finally, he decided that the safest way to travel was by the same route he had come. It was a two-day journey at a good speed. The prospect of making it with an empty stomach, tired legs, and painful feet was hardly a comforting one.

But what could he do? Even if he wanted to beg, which he did not, no one would give. Begging was forbidden, and the beggars had been rounded up and sent to working camps. Should Sung try to beg, he could be taken prisoner and sent to no-one-could-tell where. However, the boy found some relief in the thought that he could sleep in temples or at doorsteps because the weather was warm and dry. As for eating, he could perhaps ask the friendly inn-keeper of Sah-ping village, where he had stayed, to give him a free meal.

When he arrived at Sah-ping, Sung was hungrier than he had ever been in his whole life. He went directly to the inn whose owner had advised him to go on to the *hsien* city. The innkeeper happened to be outside his door in the street, trying to solicit customers, and to drag them into the inn if necessary.

"So you are back." The innkeeper greeted Sung warmly as an old friend. "Did you find the monkey circus?"

"No," Sung replied woefully.

"I'm sorry," the innkeeper said in a sympathetic voice. "Maybe you will find it some other time, or in some other place. You'll stay here tonight, of course, will you not?"

Sung hesitated.

"Please walk in," the innkeeper urged.

"I . . . I . . . must . . . tell you right now that I . . . have . . . have no money."

A dark shadow stole across the pale, shriveled features of the innkeeper, and he echoed "No money" as if he did not comprehend the meaning of these words. Then he asked, "What do you mean?"

"That I have spent all the money I had. Could you let me stay for a night and give me a bowl of rice free?"

"Free? What do you mean? I wish I could, but . . ." Without finishing what he had intended to say, he turned to a traveler with a canvas sack carried on a cane over his shoulder and ushered him toward the inn.

"I don't have to occupy a bed. I could sleep on a bench or the floor," Sung said, running after him. The innkeeper gave no indication that he had heard but went right inside with the new customer.

Sung remained standing outside the door, hoping to speak to the innkeeper again. He waited for a while, but the innkeeper did not appear. Evidently he wanted to avoid him. As though suddenly awakened, Sung said bitterly, "No use begging," and walked away. "Sleep is no problem," he told himself, "but I must eat. I cannot possibly travel two days without eating anything. But how can I find food?"

He sat down on the stone doorstep of a temple that looked much like Yui-wang-kung in his own New Market Place. There wasn't much he could do. He had no money, so he could not buy food. If he tried to steal, he would almost surely be caught and probably also be whipped, and he still wouldn't get anything to eat.

There was an eating stall right across the street from where he sat. He not only saw the bowls and dishes clearly, but he could smell the garlic and soy sauce and hot peppers and sesame oil. They stimulated his appetite and drew water to his mouth. His stomach roared and revolted. But what could he do to get some of these things into his mouth and stomach? Nothing. He thought it might be better to walk away and avoid the torture of the tempting sights and odors. So he got up and plodded off.

When he had gone ten or fifteen paces, he stopped. He hesitated for a moment, then turned back and strode directly to the eating stall. He took a seat at the long table, which was made of a door supported on two tall benches. "A large bowl of rice, a dish of bean sprouts with soy sauce and hot peppers, and a dish of bean cheese," he ordered.

The dishes of bean sprouts and molded bean curd were shoved to him. He devoured the food eagerly. No delicacy could have tasted better. When he had cleaned up every last grain of rice, he turned to the stall keeper and said bluntly, "I'm sorry to have to tell you that I have no money, and I'm a stranger here, but I'll pay you with my shirt."

The vendor stared at him dumbfounded, too angry to speak. At last he said, "*What?*"

Sung repeated what he had said.

"That dirty rag?" the stall keeper cried in a fierce

voice, pointing his greasy and sauce-stained finger at Sung's shirt. "You think it's worth a penny?"

"I cannot disgorge what I've already swallowed, even if you send me to jail."

The vendor fumed and cursed and clenched his fists and teeth as if he had been outraged. Finally, he yelled vehemently, "Strip down, you little devil."

Sung gave the vendor his shirt, the only upper garment he had, and left as quickly as he could. Now that his stomach was full, or partly full, he could look for a place to sleep. He wandered along the street, not knowing what kind of place he wanted. As the evening wore on, the temperature dropped. This, added to the bareness of his body, made him realize that it would be cold to sleep without a roof over him and without anything over his body. Fortunately, as he groped inside the temple in front of which he had been sitting a while ago, he found a pile of fresh rice straw at a corner under the stage. He was as gladdened as if he had discovered a pile of silver, and said to himself, "Ah! Heaven never shuts off all paths to a person. How true!"

He spread out a thick layer of the straw and burrowed into it. The straw irritated his bare skin, but it was no worse than the biting of bedbugs. Anyway, he was too tired to be kept awake by the irritation. Soon he was soundly asleep, and he slept until the cold air of dawn awakened him. It was just twilight, but he got up immediately and set out on his journey.

Approaching noon, hunger began tormenting

him again. His legs became heavier and heavier; his stomach groaned; his heart beat fast; even his head grew dizzy and his eyes blurred. He resorted to drinking water for relief. It made him feel better, but only momentarily.

As the sun grew hotter, his bare back and shoulders scorched. He wetted them with water from the rice fields but it did not give him much relief. Finally he broke off some leafy branches and carried them over his shoulders. Pedestrians turned back and stared at him.

When he arrived at a village and passed in front of a food stall, his hunger became insufferable. He went up to the vendor and asked for a bowl of rice congee. The vendor studied him and his bare, sunburned body suspiciously, and asked, "Do you have money?"

Sung confessed that he had spent all his money, and that he was a stranger and very hungry. "Please do me a favor?" he begged.

"I'm here doing business, not favors," the vendor said and waved him to go away.

Sung swallowed the insult, clenched his teeth, compressed his lips, and tramped on at once by sheer force of will. For a while he forgot both hunger and fatigue. He must arrive at Tai-ping village as soon as possible—the longer the time, the greater the danger of starvation for him. He could not possibly journey another day with an empty stomach; then he would never be able to reach Tai-ping village. So he summoned up all his strength and ignored the pain in his legs and feet as does a wounded soldier trying to escape being captured by the enemy.

Sung reached Tai-ping village shortly after dark, but he collapsed on the stone pavement at the mouth of the street.

A man at an adjacent house, hearing the thud, opened the door and looked out. Muttering, he went away and returned a minute later with an oil lamp.

"Ah! It's the boy Sung," he cried bending over. "What happened? Where have you been?" Sung recognized the proprietor of the teahouse, the one where he had found the coolies resting on his first arrival at the village.

"Please tell my innkeeper to come to fetch me," he implored. "I cannot walk any more."

"What's the matter? Are you ill?"

"No, I'm tired and hungry and my feet hurt terribly."

"Ah! Yes, indeed, look how thin and pale you are. I can assist you to the inn." The man put the lamp on the side of the street and helped Sung to his feet. Sung leaned on him, put his arm around his shoulders, and limped to the inn.

14 The owner of the teahouse put Sung on a bench in the lobby of the inn and called to the innkeeper. His wife answered. She hobbled in with needlework in her hands, a pair of steel-rimmed spectacles over her nose. She put her work on the table and took off the spectacles. Her eyes grew big as she inspected Sung.

"What happened?" she gasped. "An accident? Malaria again? Why, you are naked. Where's your shirt?"

"I traded it for a meal," Sung replied. "I'm hungry, please give me something to eat."

"Just hungry? Not malaria?"

"Yes, just hungry, very hungry—starving. Please give me some food at once," Sung found the strength to demand.

"Well!" The fat woman gave a sigh of relief and chuckled. "Can one be that hungry? We've had supper already, but I've some fried sticky-rice dough balls left."

"Fried sticky-rice dough balls for a starving man? No," the owner of the teahouse cried. "They'd kill him. Give him some fluid food first, such as congee."

"I can eat anything, even iron." said Sung. "Please be quick, it's gnawing at my entrails."

"Just congee now," the inkeeper's wife agreed. "I've some fresh congee cooked with bean milk. Waiter, bring him a bowl at once. I'll fetch a shirt."

The waiter brought a large bowl of lukewarm congee. Sung gulped it down in one swallow and asked for more.

"No, no more now," the innkeeper's wife said. "You shouldn't eat too much at once. Wash your feet and go to bed. I'll give you other things tomorrow morning. Waiter, fetch a basin of warm water."

When the water was brought and Sung put his feet in the basin, he screamed and drew them back.

"What's the matter? Hot?" the woman asked.

"No, it's only lukewarm," replied the waiter.

"It's not the water, it's my feet," said Sung.

The innkeeper's wife bent down and inspected his feet. "Ah! Blisters, all over," she cried, "as big as eggs. No wonder you can't walk."

Sung dipped his feet in the water slowly, and the waiter washed them for him. Clenching his teeth, Sung cried and groaned, although the man was very gentle.

"So you did not find your dog, eh?" the innkeeper's wife asked to distract him.

"No, but I've found a clue about him," Sung replied.

"Are you going to look for him any more?"

"Of course. But I'll look in a different direction, along the railroad, when we go home."

Sung could not get up to go to bed. His skin was burned and he could hardly move. His whole frame was stiff, as if paralyzed. He had to be carried to bed. He stayed there for two days before he could get up and walk again.

Then Ching Chang returned to Tai-ping village. When he learned what Sung had done, he scolded both Sung and the innkeeper's wife for the folly. "You could have starved to death," he said severely, "and we wouldn't even know where to look for your corpse."

Sung wanted to go home by hiking along the railroad so that he could look for Lucky in nearby villages, but Ching Chang flatly refused to consider it. "No more folly," he said in a tone of finality. "We'll go by train. If you must look more, you should first get your parents' permission. We've been away too long anyway. They must be worrying about you."

So they boarded a northbound train on an early morning. It was Sung's first railway trip and he should have enjoyed it enormously, but he was too busily engaged in looking out of the window for Lucky. He wondered what he should do in case he saw his little dog trotting along beside the track. He could shout and wave to him, of course, but with the train going so fast, would Lucky notice him? And even if he noticed him, then what? Lucky could not

100

jump onto the train; neither could Sung jump off it. He could get off at the next stop, but that might be a long way, and no one could tell what might happen to the dog between here and there, and between now and then. But the fact was that Sung never saw Lucky or any dog along the way—there were only bicycle-riders, wheelbarrow-pushers, coolies, farmers, children, and water buffaloes.

In a few hours the train arrived at the station nearest to New Market Place. Ching Chang and Sung got off to walk the rest of the way. Sung was suddenly aware that he would see his mother and father shortly and his heart lightened.

Soon the two found themselves on the same path that they had treaded on their trip southward, when Lucky had playfully chased the frogs and grass-hoppers in the rice fields. Now all the rice had been cut, and the fields lay dry and bare except for stacks of straw, spilled grains of rice, and stubble. The memory of Lucky came back to Sung and saddened him, and he sighed.

"What's the matter?" Ching Chang asked. "Is it the dog? You should be very happy that Lucky has found a good master, if he is actually with a monkey circus. The dog hunters will not kill a dog that per-forms in a circus."

Sung plodded on gloomily without replying and with his head bent.

They walked quietly, until they had climbed to the top of a knoll and the tower of Yui-wang-kung came to view. Then Ching Chang said, "There is no place like dear old New Market Place. I like it more than Canton."

"I like my home more than any place I've seen," Sung said. "How I have missed my father and mother! But I will be seeing them soon!" And he quickened his steps.

Ching Chang asked suddenly, "Do you hear a droning noise from New Market Place?"

Sung stopped and listened. "I forgot," he cried out. "It's a market day at New Market Place. Maybe there's a monkey circus in town!" At once he started to run, his bare feet flashing in the bright sunlight.

"There's no need for hurrying," Ching Chang said. "If the circus is there, it will be there for quite a while yet."

But Sung had run far ahead. Ching Chang shouted to him, "Wait for me at Wu's eating house. We'll have a farewell dinner before we go home."

There was no reply from Sung. He ran all the way to New Market Place, only to slow down at the mouth of the street because it was crammed with a line of slowly moving people. He could hear the sound of a gong, the kind beaten by monkey-circus men, from inside Yui-wang-kung. It excited him to the point of delirium. He pushed and shoved, and ignored the complaints and curses of those he bumped against.

The courtyard of the temple was boiling with the clatter of bells and confused shouting, as well as the sound of the gong which came from the corner where the coffins stood. A dense crowd had gathered there. The people were cheering and laughing. Sung knew for sure it must be a monkey circus. He moved around the human wall in search of a peep-hole but found none. The spectators were crowded too tightly.

Then he heard the circus man's shout, "Come on, now, Lucky! Let's go."

Sung's heart raced. He leaped into the air, but he only caught a glimpse of the circus man, not the monkey or the dog. He made another circle around the crowd. At one point he found two long, mud-coated legs set wide apart on straw-sandaled feet. Sung crouched on his knees, put his head between the legs, and, before the owner of the legs knew what was happening, he had bored into the human ring and popped up right in the front row beside a low railing.

He saw Lucky! It was *his* Lucky, with coal-black fur, snow-white paws, and a white-tipped tail!

15 When Sung saw Lucky, he nearly shouted out loud. Although he restrained himself and watched quietly, he was shaking with emotion and had to fight back tears.

Lucky was pulling a tiny wooden plow, which the monkey held. The monkey wore a toylike rain hat of woven bamboo and a sleeveless red shirt and carried a bamboo branch for a whip. The dog was acting the role of the water buffalo; the monkey the role of the farmer. They were walking in a circle. As they moved along, the monkey guided the plow left and right like a farmer. Now and then he would wave his whip at the dog, just as a farmer does to the water buffalo. But Lucky seemed to be performing passively, spiritlessly. His tail drooped.

The circus man stopped the gong and shouted, "Halt!" Lucky and the monkey stood still while the circus man unharnessed Lucky and put the plow beside a large basket.

104

"Now let's have another stunt," he said to the monkey, and gave him a pat on the head. "You will not be plowing a field but riding a donkey. This is your donkey." He pointed at Lucky. "You are a jockey, a country squire. Understand? Mount him and let us see what a wonderful rider you are."

The monkey did not budge.

"Come on, let's go," said the man.

The monkey acted as if he had not heard.

"What's the matter with you? Do you hear me? Are you bashful? Are you timid? Don't you know how to ride?"

The monkey still ignored his command.

The circus man gave a dry laugh and said, "I know what's the matter with you, you rascal. You want money. People pay money to have a ride, but you want to be paid to ride, you bad boy! Gentlemen," he lifted his head to the spectators, "please kindly open your generous purses and bestow upon the greedy beggar more money." He took a small shallow basket out of the large one and began to collect money from the audience. When he had completed the round, he showed the little basket to the monkey and said, "Now here's your money. Let's go."

The monkey glanced at the contents of the basket but remained standing still.

"What's the idea?" the circus man said with feigned anger. "The gentlemen have given you more money and you *still* refuse to perform? I'll give the money back."

105

The monkey screamed and grabbed at the basket, then became immovable again.

"What do you mean? You don't want to perform, and you don't want to give the money back?" The circus man gave another dry laugh and said, "Oh, I know. He is a spoiled little monkey, spoiled by generous patrons. He wants *more* money. Gentlemen, won't you dig deeper into your pockets? I'll thrash him if he still refuses to act."

More money was collected. The circus man showed it to the monkey, who looked at it and then leaped upon the dog's back. The man beat the gong; Lucky started to walk. But he walked slowly and languidly, his tail down. It was obvious that he did not enjoy the stunt as much as the monkey did.

"Go faster," the man said.

The dog kept the same pace.

"Make him go faster," the man said to the monkey.

The little animal brandished his whip over the dog's back. Lucky raised his head and started to move at a trot. Just as he completed one round and drew near to where Sung stood, his ears pricked forward and his tail began to wave. His trot suddenly changed to a gallop and Lucky leaped forward, throwing the monkey to the ground.

As if he had gone mad, the little dog jumped over the railing and landed in Sung's arms. Barking and whimpering, he pressed his head tightly against Sung's neck and face.

"Lucky! My Lucky!" Sung moaned. He held the dog securely with both hands and rubbed his cheek

106

against the soft fur.

The astonished spectators turned their heads and stared, dumbfounded. The circus man, who had stopped the gong, stood in the middle of the ring as if petrified. The monkey sat on the floor beside his master. He turned his tiny, bewildered face from the dog to the man and back to the dog again, as though demanding an explanation of what was happening.

"It's *my* dog," Sung declared at last.

"*Your* dog?" the circus man snapped. "You must be out of your mind!"

"But the dog cannot be out of *his* mind," Sung replied.

"That's right," several spectators agreed.

The circus man straddled forward and, snatching Lucky from Sung's arms, held him on the ground. "*Your* dog!" he repeated and spat. "I paid three hard silver dollars for him. I bought him from three boys down south at a place near the long railway tunnel."

The three boys who had carried the water for them! Now Sung understood how the circus man had learned his dog's real name.

"That's where I lost him," Sung said. "Let me have him back and I'll refund your three dollars."

"You shall not have him back," a loud voice said from behind Sung, and the boy felt two powerful hands seize his arms. Twisting around, Sung was amazed to see Ching Chang.

"Let them perform and let us go to eat," the pig

107

drover commanded. He pulled Sung away from the crowd and dragged him toward the street.

The sound of the gong and the shouts of the circus man resumed, and the spectators were soon laughing again.

Sung let himself be pulled along. He did not know what he felt. When they came to the gate of the temple, he said to Ching Chang, "Will you lend me three dollars?"

"To redeem Lucky?" his friend said sharply. "That man will not sell the dog for ten times three dollars. Don't you see Lucky is indispensable to him? There can be no monkey show without the dog, and he cannot possibly find another dog to take Lucky's place."

"Then how can I get him back?"

"Why do you want to get him back?" Ching Chang snapped. "You want him to be killed? Why did you go south with me? Wasn't it to give Lucky away, to find a safe place and a master for him? Now that, by a strange chance, he has found the ideal master and is safe, you want to have him back. Isn't that a crazy idea? It is much better to lose him this way than by turning him loose in Hong Kong where he might never be able to find a home. You know he will always be safe in the circus! What is the matter with you?"

When Sung did not answer, Ching Chang went on, more kindly, "The monkey show will come to our village or our neighborhood from time to time, so you will be able to see Lucky once in a while.

What could be better?"

Sung still said nothing. He could not fail to see the truth of what Ching Chang had said, but neither could he rid himself of his longing for Lucky.

They arrived at Wu's inn and eating house and sat down at a table in front of the door. After ordering, Ching Chang laid his stout arms on the table before him, his fingers interlocked, and resumed in a whisper, "I am awfully happy to find Lucky in the possession of a circus man. Not one dog in a million *is* so lucky. Can you figure out how the circus man got him?"

"He said he bought him from three boys," Sung replied. "But I don't know how those boys got hold of him."

"Ah, I can guess," Ching Chang said. "When Lucky saw the train rush into the tunnel, he must have turned and run the other way. You see, he was smart, much smarter than the pigs. He probably got outside the tunnel ahead of the train. Then the three boys captured him. Fortunately, they did not kill him and eat his meat. They must have hidden him away until they found the circus man."

"I think you must be right," Sung said, as the waiter brought the dishes of food, and he began to realize how lucky his Lucky had been. He must not spoil that luck. But still he just had to be with his dog again. "I am not going to reclaim him," Sung said slowly, at last, "but I must bring him home, if just for a few minutes, for my parents to see him."

"Why must you bring him home for them to see?

109

Don't you realize that the minute he is out of the circus man's hands he would be in danger of getting killed by any soldier you happened to meet? Why don't you ask your parents to come to see him, to watch him perform and see what a wonderful circus actor he has become? They'll be pleased, certainly."

"Not a bad idea," Sung cried, excited at the thought of showing off Lucky. He quickly finished his meal, then thanked Ching Chang and said good-bye. He hopped and danced along the narrow, slate-paved path, down which a few months ago on a cold and drizzling February morning, Lucky, then a tiny puppy, had followed him home. Sung wondered whether the puppy had not been directed by some mysterious guiding hand to its safety. His mother had named him Lucky; Sung thought she had been wise. Halfway home a song formed in his head, and he began to sing aloud as he hopped and danced:

> Lucky, monkey, donkey, and jockey,
> Lucky's acting as a donkey,
> The jockey's only a monkey.
> Oh, poor Lucky,
> Who's riding on your back?
> He's not a real jockey
> But a naughty little monkey.
> Oh, poor Lucky.

16 When Sung came to the edge of the threshing yard where the shaddock tree stood, he shouted out excitedly, "Father, Mother, I am home! I have news for you! Lucky has become a circus actor and is now performing at Yui-wang-kung. Come to see him." He had to pause to catch his breath before he shouted again.

He had crossed the yard and ascended the terrace, intending to go directly to the kitchen, when he noticed that the door of the middle room was wide open and many people were inside. He wondered who they were and what they were doing there. Then he saw that they were eating at a large round table. He was surprised because his family had only a square table, not a round one.

Why were so many guests at his home, Sung wondered. Was it some festival, the birthday of his father or mother? He quickly realized that it was not. He stopped in front of the door and hesitated. The faces inside were all unfamiliar—faces that belonged to city people, not country folk. Sung looked for his father and mother, but neither was there. The boy was stunned, unmindful of the eyes that were staring at him. He boldly stepped across the high doorsill and shuffled to the room on the left, where his parents slept.

A tall, pale-skinned man in a white shirt stalked up to him, arms akimbo, tapped him on the shoulder from behind, and inquired in a none-too-polite voice, "Sir, may I ask what you are looking for?"

"I'm looking for my parents. Where are they?"

"Who are your parents? What makes you think they are here?"

"This is our home, and this is their room."

"Oh, I see now," the man said, his face more relaxed. "You are looking for the people who used to live here? But they have moved out. This house has been assigned to our use."

"Moved out?" Sung hardly understood what the man meant. He cast a quick glance around the room and became more bewildered, because it was crammed with cots and bedding, boxes and baskets that did not belong to his family, while the possessions of his family had disappeared. He walked into the room on the right, which had been his. It also was piled with cots, boxes, and suitcases unfamiliar to him. For a moment, he thought he was dreaming. He gave his head a vigorous shake and looked around. Everything was real and unmistakable—the people; the dishes and bowls on the table with vapor rising from them; the faded door gods; the bright sunlight falling across the patched, packed-earth floor; the deserted front yard; and the shaddock tree, on which the fruits had grown almost yellow and ripe. Sung could even smell the food the people were eating, and the tobacco they were smoking. No, it was not a dream!

"Where have my parents moved to?" he asked as he returned to the middle room, without addressing the question to any person in particular.

"How do we know?" several voices replied at the same time. Then one of them added, "We were sent here by the Provincial Government to help increase food production. This house had been vacated before we moved in. You have to find out from the local *hsiang* government."

Sung plodded out of the house with a bent head, utterly lost, not knowing what to do or where to go. When he came to the shaddock tree at the edge of the threshing yard, he sat down on a stone and tried to figure out what it all meant. Slowly he realized that he had found his dog but had lost his parents. The dog was supposed to be lucky but had brought calamity to Sung's family instead! The boy burst into a sob. Floods of tears gushed out of his eyes. He covered his face with his hands and wept miserably. He shed so many tears that the sleeves of his shirt became as wet as its back.

Finally, he got up and dragged his steps toward New Market Place. The *hsiang*, or commune, office was overflowing both with people and with noise. Heaps of bedrolls, boxes, and baskets cluttered the

113

courtyard. Sung learned that the people here, like his parents, were to be expatriated to other districts. He attached himself to the long line, and waited his turn to speak to the clerk of the office.

"What is your father's name?" the clerk demanded in an accented voice. Apparently he came from a northern province. Then, brows knit, he thumbed through a thick and much grimed ledger, moistening his fingers frequently in his mouth. Finally, he jabbed a finger at a spot in the middle of a page and said, "There they are. Your father is undertaking earthwork in Po-yang Lake; your mother is working in a cotton mill in Hankow."

"How is it that they are not in the same place?" Sung asked, bewildered.

"They don't do the same type of work," the clerk replied curtly.

"How can I find them?"

"You can find your mother at the First Cotton Mill of Central China in Hankow, but I don't see how you can find your father at Po-yang Lake, because there are some three hundred thousand people working there at the same project and no one knows who works and stays where."

"When will he come home?"

"He may not return here for a long time. When the work at Po-yang Lake is finished, he may be assigned to some other project, such as building a highway in Tibet or a railroad in Inner Mongolia." With these words, the official shut the book with a clap and turned to the next person in the line.

114

Sung walked away helplessly. He had no idea where Hankow city was, or Po-yang Lake, and how far. He did not know what to do and where to go. He leaned against the wall of the *hsiang* office near the door like a statue. He was not crying any more; he had exhausted his tears. Finally, it occurred to him that he should go to see Ching Chang. He trudged out of the *hsiang* office and out of New Market Place with stooped head. Just a short distance from the mouth of the village, at the place where he had first found the three abandoned puppies about half a year ago, he encountered Ching Chang. The latter had changed to a clean white shirt and new straw sandals, and looked washed and refreshed. "I was coming to see you at your home, my boy," he said in a soft, kindly voice, "when I learned that your parents had been sent away. Do you know where they are?"

"Yes . . ." Sung was choked by tears. He clenched his teeth to fight them back; then went on, "Hankow, and Po-yang Lake, but I . . . I have . . . no idea . . . where those places are."

"They are far, you have to go by train or steamer." Ching Chang groped in his shirt pocket, produced a small package wrapped in coarse yellow paper, and handed it to Sung. "Your mother left this with my wife for you. She said that you may sell it and use the money to travel to her. But I don't think it's enough."

Sung opened the package with shaking hands. It contained the silver hairpin she had meant to give him for the trip to Canton and Hong Kong. He could not restrain his tears any more, and they overflowed like the Yellow River and dampened the yellowish paper that wrapped the hairpin. "Oh, Mother!" he wept. "What a kind and generous mother!"

"Stop crying, my boy," Ching Chang reprimanded. "Your mother is not dead; neither is your father. They have merely moved to other places and are working. Your mother may be earning a good wage in Hankow, because the factory workers are paid more than farm hands. She will remit you money; then you can travel to Hankow by train or steamer."

Sung became quiet, and at last his tear-stained face beamed in a smile of surprise and wonder. He looked up at Ching Chang and asked, "Are you sure she'll send me the money?"

"Why do you ask such a stupid question?" Ching Chang snapped. "Do you think that your mother will abandon her only child?"

Sung mused for a moment or two; then, wiping his eyes and face with the back of his hands, muttered, "But where can I stay before going to Hankow?"

"Right here on this roadside," Ching Chang replied with feigned severity. But then he smiled and said, "With us, of course. You can stay with us as long as you need to. But let me keep the hairpin for you so it won't be lost."

116

17 One warm, damp afternoon, Sung was helping Ching Chang with the harvest of his late rice, delayed on account of the trip to Canton. Several baskets, half filled with the harvested crop, stood in the field amidst bundles of rice straw that had been cut and threshed. Overhead, clumps of dark clouds were gathering near the sun, cutting off its slanting beams of light but not its heat. Sung was threshing the rice on a large wooden tub that had a bamboo mat screen raised around three sides to prevent the rice from scattering. Ching Chang was doing the cutting with a short-handled scythe, his large frame bending double at the waist. Sweat was streaming down their faces and bare bodies, for they were rushing to clear off a corner of the field before the storm broke.

A diminutive, elderly man approached along the stone-paved path and, waving his hand, called in a high-pitched voice, "Sung, Sung . . . "

"What is it?" Ching Chang, who was closer to him, demanded impatiently.

"I want to speak to the boy," the man replied.

Ching Chang turned to Sung and shouted, "It's the town crier. He wants to speak to you, over there." He pointed with the scythe.

"What is it?" Sung rushed up, surprised at the sight of the town crier.

"Don't worry," the man replied. "It's not official business; it's only that the circus man wants to see you."

"The circus man? What does he want of me?"

"How do I know? He has been looking all over for you. It must be something important; otherwise he would not have paid me a dollar to bring you the message." The town crier turned away even before he finished.

"But wait!" Sung shouted. "You haven't told me where he's staying."

"At Wu's inn, of course. That's the only inn New Market Place has."

As the town crier strode away, Ching Chang said, "He wants to sell you the dog, I think."

"Sell me Lucky? But I have no money to buy him."

"Maybe he wants to give him back to you; maybe he was moved by the tender attachment between the two of you. But that's silly! What could you do with the dog even if you had the money, or if he wanted to give it to you? The dog killers would be after it at once."

Despite these remarks, Ching Chang urged Sung to carry home the threshed rice and go to see the monkey-circus man promptly. "We can't finish anyway," he said, looking up at the dark clouds. "We had better carry home what we have already done, before it gets soaked by the rain. Take a lantern and a rain hat with you."

When Sung arrived at Wu's inn, a tall, mustached cook-waiter was standing upon a bench, lighting the large rectangular lantern outside the entrance with a lit paper spill. As he blew out the spill and stepped down, he said, "Ah, you've come! He's been expecting you. Sit down here and I'll call him." He wiped the bench with his palm and then wiped his hand on the apron.

"Sung's here," he shouted toward a room that had a latticed and paper-covered window. "The boy's here."

"I've heard you," a loud voice replied, and presently a rather small, middle-aged man with a cane-like pipe in his mouth emerged from the room. He marched briskly past the sky-well—a large, square-shaped, stone-lined hole in the ground, open to the sky, for dumping refuse and used water—and approached Sung, saying, "You are the former owner of Lucky, are you not? I must confess that I hardly recognize you, or knew your honorable name the other day at Yui-wang-kung. Things were in such confusion."

That was exactly what Sung could have said. He had retained hardly any impression of the circus man, because his attention had been completely occupied by Lucky. Now Sung studied him. The circus man had sharp eyes, a short, three-pronged beard, and a clear, forceful voice, the right kind of man for his kind of business, thought Sung.

"I've tried hard to find you," the circus man went on as he pulled up a bench and sat down beside Sung. "I neither knew your name nor your address, or anything else about you. I inquired and inquired. Well, I'm delighted that you've deigned to come. Do you smoke?" He offered his pipe, which Sung declined.

"Here!" The man turned to the tall waiter, who was splitting a large pumpkin on a table. "Buy me two bowls of tea from the teahouse across the street, and a couple of ounces of peanut-sesame candy."

He turned back to Sung, explaining somewhat needlessly, "They don't serve tea in these small country inns, but only food, you know. Now, I've got a problem. Lucky won't act properly. He sits with downcast head and walks with a drooping tail. I've tried to persuade him, coax him, and even spank him, but he only performs languidly, without spirit. The onlookers get disgusted and go away. Some say that he is pretending, like the monkey, in order to induce the audience to give more money. But it's not that, not at all. I know what it is. He misses you. Now you must speak quietly, lest he hear you and make a scene! I need your assistance. I want you to travel with me for a while, until Lucky gets used to me. I would be happy to pay all your traveling expenses, plus a small wage. Will you kindly consent?"

This offer came to Sung as an utter surprise. The prospect of traveling with the monkey-circus troupe and watching Lucky perform elated him. But he checked himself and managed to keep a cool appearance. Then he replied falteringly, "Well, I'm sorry to hear that Lucky is not doing very well. I wish I could help you, but I've work to do on the farm. We are harvesting the rice just now."

"Any person with a pair of hands can harvest rice," the circus man said contemptuously, "but you are the only one who can revive my circus. I will pay you adequately so your parents can hire someone to do the harvesting."

"My parents are away. I'm living with a friend. I'll talk it over with him. How long and how far do you want me to travel?"

They were interrupted by the waiter, who came in with two covered bowls of tea and a small package of candy wrapped in coarse paper. The circus man offered a bowl of the tea and the candy to Sung and resumed, "I have no fixed itinerary and am free to go any place, wherever there's an audience and money. I would want you to travel with me for at least ten or fifteen days, until Lucky can do without you. But if you like, well—" He stopped to sip the tea, and then picked up a piece of candy and put it between his bearded lips. Chewing, he went on, "I'm contemplating a new adventure. You see, I'm not making much money in the villages nowadays, so I would like to move on to a big city."

"Canton?"

"No, Wu-han—Hankow—the largest city in central China."

Sung started at the mention of Hankow, but he managed to maintain his calm, at least outwardly. To conceal his excitement, he picked up the tea and sipped and sipped until he recovered his composure. Then he said, "Hankow is far. You have to go by train and steamer, which would cost a great deal of money."

"But I wouldn't travel by train and steamer. I always travel on foot, and occasionally by wheelbarrow or ricksha, so I can give shows and earn money as I go. You want to know how much I would pay you? Well, I'll be straightforward with you. I am the owner of the business, and I direct the performances, so it's only fair that I should have a larger share of the earnings. I'll take fifty per cent; the remainder to be divided equally among you, the monkey, and the dog. I don't mean to put you in the same category with the monkey and the dog as you are a human being, but they are the actors who actually attract the audience and earn the money."

Sung could not figure out exactly what his share would be, not right away, so he remained silent.

The circus man resumed, "But your food and lodging would be guaranteed; that is to say, no matter how little we earn, or even if we don't earn anything at all, your lodgings and meals would be paid. Does that sound fair to you?"

"I'll talk it over with my elder," Sung replied.

Actually, Sung was enthusiastically interested and had already made up his mind to go to Hankow with the circus. He would go even if Ching Chang objected. He returned to his friend's home almost running, extremely elated and swinging the lantern high. About halfway, the lantern caught fire, because he had swung it too violently, so he threw it into the ditch at the side of the path. Now he walked slowly in the darkness. After a while, when his eyes had adjusted to the dark, he resumed his speed. The footpath was straight and level most of the way, and Sung was familiar with it, so he had no trouble.

Ching Chang opened the door for him and asked, "Where's your lantern?"

Sung ignored the question and went right on to tell Ching Chang the good news about the trip to Hankow. Having listened quietly and asked several questions, Ching Chang said, "Do go, by all means. It's a piece of luck brought you by Lucky. You wouldn't be able to find such good luck even if you had searched everywhere with lanterns and torches."

"I don't think he should travel to such a far place with a stranger," his wife objected. She was mending her husband's trousers before the tiny flame of an oil lamp and had been listening to the conversation attentively. She was a tiny woman, alert both in mind and body. She had once had a boy of her own, but he had died of dysentery at the age of six, and she had not given birth to any more children. She was fond of Sung, and had offered to escort him to

123

Hankow herself so that she might see the city.

"People like the circus man drift from place to place like flower petals in a stream," she went on. "Besides, how can you travel such a long way on foot? No one has ever done so. You might get sick, or some accident might happen. Remember the malaria on your last trip? This time of the year it's dysentery . . ."

"Oh, you are being pessimistic," her husband cut her short. "One can get sick or killed at home. However," he turned to Sung, "she has made one good point. In case the circus man abandons you in the course of the journey, what would you do?"

"No, he can't, and he won't," Sung replied. "He needs me, and his troupe is too conspicuous to hide."

"I am not so sure," Ching Chang's wife said triumphantly. "You may starve, as you almost did on your last trip."

Ching Chang began to pace the room with his hands behind his back. "Yes, here's a loophole," he murmured thoughtfully. "We must find a way to stop it. We can't take such a big chance."

"He simply shouldn't go with that man; that's all there's to it." His wife's attitude grew resolute.

Ching Chang waved a hand at her to be quiet and said, "You don't go fasting because you hiccup, as the saying goes. But we must have a hold on that man so that in case . . . just in case . . . ah! I have it. We'll make him pay some money in advance, say fifteen or twenty dollars, as a deposit."

"Wise idea!" both his wife and Sung cried.

It was Ching Chang who later persuaded the circus man to pay Sung twelve dollars in advance, but his wife took great pride in the accomplishment because it was an outgrowth of her suggestion. When the money was brought home, she said to Sung, "Of course you should take the money with you against mishaps during travel. Have you thought how to carry it?"

"In my pocket, of course," replied Sung.

"That's simple enough. But have you thought of the pickpockets, or that you might lose it through carelessness?"

Sung realized the risk and was silent.

Ching Chang's wife had a plan on her mind. She made a small bag, put the money and the silver hairpin in it, and sewed the bag inside the pocket of his jacket. "Don't you ever part with the jacket," she admonished in a whisper, gazing intently into Sung's eyes to impress him. "Always put it on in daytime; when you go to bed, put it under your pillow. You hear me?"

Sung nodded, with a little smile. It was apparent that he thought her warning superfluous.

"You hear me?" she repeated with a grave face.

"Yes, I hear you," Sung replied, in the voice and manner of a soldier to a general.

18 Sung's trip to Hankow with the monkey circus had hardly anything in common with his trip to Canton with the pig dealer. In the first place, the weather was mild, while during the first trip it had been terribly hot. Secondly, there was no need to worry about the dog's being discovered and killed. Thirdly, Sung did not have to endure the stink of the pigs which sometimes had made him feel nauseated. True, he had to carry the monkey, a condition imposed by the circus man when Ching Chang demanded the payment of the advance money from him. But the little monkey was scarcely heavier than a newborn baby. Moreover, he did not have to be carried all the time. He walked a lot, or he would jump upon Lucky's back and ride. Once in a while, he would leap on Sung's shoulder, perch there, and scratch his hair, searching for lice, which always tickled Sung. No, the little monkey did not constitute a burden at all; rather he made the journey more interesting, or at least less wearisome.

As Sung watched the circus man slowly walking along, his back somewhat stooped under the weight of his belongings and the props of the show which he carried in a large bamboo basket, with his long pipe tucked in a sash at his hip, he realized how absurd it was to suspect that this man could run away from him and forsake him. What pleased Sung especially was that the circus man was a great talker and an interesting storyteller. He would tell story after story from his own experience until he became exhausted from the walking, when they would stop and give a show. Sometimes he would hire a wheelbarrow, and they would ride on it, humans, monkey, and dog. On the highways there were rickshas for hire; they would hire two, and the circus man rode on one with the luggage, while Sung rode on the other with the monkey and the dog. Often

Sung would refuse to ride and would run along beside the ricksha with Lucky, letting the circus man ride with the monkey, because he was older.

They seldom traveled more than thirty or forty *li* each day, depending on opportunities for performance, their mood, and other circumstances such as the weather. They performed most days, though sometimes only once every other day. The performances were routine—the circus man beat the gong to attract a crowd; the monkey began with somersaults, then put on the red shirt, took up the whip, and rode on Lucky's back; the circus man hitched the little toy plow to Lucky, and the monkey started plowing. The whole show didn't take more than fifteen or twenty minutes, depending on how fast the spectators contributed the money. Then the same stunts would be repeated and more money collected. They didn't make much, but cleared enough to pay their expenses. The circus man never complained. He said that the place to make real money was Hankow.

Sung found the journey more interesting after the second day, because the places were unfamiliar to him. They traveled mostly on narrow footpaths, though once in a while along highways. Few motor vehicles were seen on the highways; often none for hours. Whenever such vehicles did come, they drove fast and stirred up heavy clouds of dust, or, what was worse, sprays of mud. But the highways were not idle—there were always bicycles, rickshas, pedicabs, wheelbarrows, and pedestrians that served to remind Sung of the traffic along the railroad on his last trip.

The terrain they traveled was mostly flat—paddy fields now mostly dry and bare after the harvest, dotted with ponds of clear water and patches of other crops. A common object in the ponds were the water buffaloes. They stayed immersed in the water, showing only their huge horns and big, fearful eyes, contented and motionless except to blink at the flies that lighted on them. Once in a while the travelers would pass small lakes. More than just water reservoirs and fisheries, water crops such as lotus, water chestnuts, taro, and reeds were grown in them.

Sung had lost track of the date. All he could figure out was that they had been on the road more than a month, because the new moon had grown full, then waned, then disappeared, and had now returned. One afternoon, they saw a cluster of hills in the distance, and Sung asked the circus man whether he knew their name.

"Don't you know the famous Lu-shan?" the circus man retorted. "They are among the most famous mountains in the whole country."

"They don't look so big."

"But they are very famous. Many high officials and rich people and foreigners from Shanghai, Nanking, and Hankow have summer homes up there. Chiang Kai-shek used to spend the summer months there every year. Many important conferences were held there, including the one where it was decided to fight the Japanese. At present the Communists also hold frequent meetings there. Didn't you know these things?"

His words and the tone in which they were spoken made Sung conscious of his ignorance. The boy became silent and somber. The circus man noticed this, so he changed his tone and added, "We are going up there tomorrow, so you will see some of the places of interest. Maybe we can give a performance or two and earn some money."

The next day they arrived at Ku-ling, the residential center on the top of Lu-shan, just before noon. It was a community mostly of Western-style bungalows, hotels, restaurants, and office buildings. Many of them were closed, and there were few people around. The circus man sighed and lamented. "We are just a little too late; summer is over and they are all gone."

The circus man took Sung around and showed him the historical and scenic places, including the house where Chiang Kai-shek had lived. Sung was not impressed, because it looked no different from other houses except that it was a little larger. He preferred the creeks with their clear gurgling water, the little waterfalls and the blue pools below them, the wildflowers and wild berries. He especially loved the several giant trees on the premises of a temple; he had not thought that trees could grow that big and tall.

As they wound through the narrow, bush-lined trail to the outer side of the hill, they came upon a

130

panoramic view of the valley below. The vast openness made Sung gasp. There lay under their feet a long and broad band of pale yellow water glimmering in the sun—the mighty Yangtze River, that meanders to the limitless horizon and disappears as though emptying its contents into the heavens. On one side of the river spread another extensive body of water, that could be likened to a stomach, if the Yangtze was the intestine. Just as Sung was going to ask what that body of water was, the circus man lifted his long pipe and, pointing said, "There's the Po-yang Lake . . ."

"Po-yang! Did you say Po-yang?" Sung cried.

"Yes, Po-yang, one of the largest lakes of China."

"Are we going there?"

"No, there's nothing interesting at the lake, just muddy water."

"But my father is working there! I would like to see him."

The circus man fixed his sharp eyes on the boy with a puzzled look and said, "You know how many people are working there? Half a million! You can't possibly find a single individual in such a crowd."

"Only three hundred thousand," Sung said, remembering what the clerk at New Market Place had told him.

"That wouldn't make much difference. Three hundred thousand persons scattered over a vast territory! And what are you going to do to find him? Run around and holler 'Daddy'? They would all think you are crazy." And he burst into laughter, the first time Sung had seen him laugh.

Sung could not help seeing the point, so he did not press the argument. But neither could he help feeling a sense of frustration. He had unexpectedly come close to the place where his father was working; yet he could not go there.

At the same time, the circus man was by no means in high spirits. After so much climbing, which tired him much more than it did Sung, he had not earned a penny. So, as they descended the hills that late afternoon, few words were exchanged between them. They went to bed earlier than usual and omitted the bedtime conversation, which they normally carried on until the lamp was blown out.

The following morning the circus man surprised Sung by announcing that he had changed his mind about a detour to the lake. "So many people in there, and they work without play," he observed with cheerfulness. "Maybe they would love a little diversion and even be willing to pay a few coppers for it. As for seeing your father, maybe you'll have the most unusual luck, like one who wins first prize in a lottery."

Close as the lake had looked from the hill, it took them several hours to reach its nearest corner. Spread before them, as far as, and even farther than, their eyes could see, were myriads of human ants bustling around. At closer look, they were found to be digging and shoveling sand and mud into baskets, carrying the baskets on their shoulders five hundred or a thousand paces away, and dumping them. As the circus man and Sung sauntered past them, some of them cast curious glances at the monkey and the dog. Others even stopped working for a moment and smiled at them.

"They are dredging the lake," the circus man said to Sung.

"A tremendous amount of work," the boy replied.

"They are just crazy," the circus man said in a lower voice, glancing furtively around to see if anyone was within earshot. "I mean, the authorities who make these people toil here are crazy."

"Why?"

"Because all that these hundreds of thousands of people can accomplish in months can be and will be undone by the river in a few hours. You see how muddy the water is. It's even muddier in the summer."

Sung was chewing these words to extract their meaning when the circus man went on, "You wonder how I know such things? My family have lived in the vicinity of Po-yang for generations, out there." He pointed with his pipe toward the far side of the lake where houses could be seen faintly gleaming under clumps of white clouds. "When they came to our village to recruit workers, we told them that they would be wasting the people's time. You know what they said? They laughed and swore that armed with Chairman Mao's thought there's no difficulty but can be overcome. They recited the legendary story of an old man who tried to move a hill because

it was in his way. When he was told that he was attempting the impossible, the old man replied, 'The hill does not grow, but my family will multiply. Although I cannot finish the job, my children, their children, and their children's children will do the work after me, so eventually the task will be accomplished.' That may well be, theoretically, though I don't believe that the old man's children and their children will perpetuate his work and finish it. But anyway the lake is a different phenomenon. It does grow, and grows fast. Floods come every year and unload millions of tons of sand and silt. You have to go upstream to do the things that can reduce the silt content of the water and lower the flood level . . . but let's go over there, and see if we

134

can find a place to make a little money."

The circus man was pointing to the bottom of a
foothill where stonemasons were quarrying with
hammers swung by hand, while hordes of carriers in
teams of two or four were moving the stones down
to the edge of the lake for the construction of a dike.
He stopped at a piece of level ground midway between the quarry and the site of the dike, just off the
path of the stone carriers. Then he beat the gong.
The crowd began to collect, empty baskets on their
shoulders. Some of the stonemasons stopped ham-
mering and chanting. The earth diggers also paused
and, leaning on their hoes and shovels, looked up.
The circus man ordered the monkey to do somersaults. The crowd laughed and applauded.

Just then, a smallish young man in a Mao tunic and visored cap ran up from the site of the dike and, catching his breath, demanded, "What's going on here?"

All became quiet. The crowd stopped laughing, and the monkey stopped jumping. The young man swept the crowd with a pair of frightening eyes; then he caught sight of the monkey, the dog, and the circus man with the gong in his hand.

"I see, a monkey show! Get you off! This is not the place and time for amusement." He struck the ground with the cane he carried and turned to the crowd, shouting, "Go back to work."

The crowd at once dispersed. Just then Lucky barked at the young man, and the man raised his cane at the dog. Sung pulled Lucky back, but Lucky barked louder and bared his teeth.

The young man drew his pistol. Sung quickly picked up Lucky in his arms and carried him away, running as if fleeing for his own life.

"Who's he?" Sung asked the circus man, when they were alone and at a safe distance from the official with the cane and the pistol.

"The supervisor, and a member of the Communist party," the circus man replied in a low voice, though they were far from earshot of any other person. "We could have been flogged or arrested if we tried to quarrel with him."

"My fault," Sung said. "I shouldn't have persuaded you to come. I'm convinced now that I cannot possibly find my father in this place."

136

19 As long as he was on the way to Hankow to visit his mother and busily occupied with the monkey show and other activities, Sung's longing for his parents remained dormant, although he had been separated from them for so long. Now that he had unexpectedly run into Po-yang Lake where his father worked, his longing was suddenly reawakened and became difficult to bear. The boy realized that he had been traveling for many days and that his mother must be expecting him anxiously. He also faced up to the fact that he had to part with Lucky sooner or later, much as he regretted it. Fortunately, Lucky had found a good master, even an occupation. Sung could not have disposed of the dog in a better way. He further realized that, as Lucky and the circus man had become good friends, he was no longer indispensable to the show.

These thoughts kept him awake the night after the trip to Po-yang Lake. He heard the circus man snore, turn his body, and even mutter some indistinct words, apparently while dreaming. He also heard the dog groan in a low voice and scratch himself from time to time. But Sung lay in bed wide awake and thinking. His mind seemed all the more clear in the quietness of night. The steamers that he had seen going up and down the river in the daytime returned to his vision vividly, and he said to himself, "Why not take a steamer and get to Hankow in a day? Why spend fifteen days walking, as the circus man has planned?"

The circus-man's bed creaked. He coughed and got up. Then he struck a match and lit the lamp and, carrying it, shuffled out of the room. Sung did not stir. A few minutes later, the circus man returned from the outhouse, and as he put the lamp on the table, Sung sat up.

"Do you want to go out there?" the circus man asked sleepily.

"No, but I want to talk to you . . ."

"Talk! At this hour? What about? Go back to sleep, you can talk all you want tomorrow."

"But it's something urgent. Can we go to Hankow by steamer?"

"Why? We've agreed to walk and perform all the way to Hankow, haven't we? We're just coming to a richer and more populous area, and I'm hoping to earn some money."

"My mother must have been expecting me for a long time. She must be worried. I'm feeling all upset, and I can't be of help to you when my mind is so unsettled."

"Let's go to sleep and talk tomorrow." The circus man blew out the lamp and slipped into his quilt.

Sung remained awake for a long time, thinking. He made up his mind to take a steamer to Hankow even if he had to do it alone. He wouldn't have to ask for money; he had enough money in his pocket for the trip.

The following morning the circus man got up first. He awakened Sung and told him that he had thought over the question that had been raised last night. He could not change his plans. "But I understand why you are so impatient about seeing your mother. I love filial children, so I'll let you go by steamer, and will pay your fare. But I want you to do me a favor. You must take leave of us quietly, casually, not sentimentally. Understand? Just as if you were going out for a walk or something. Don't arouse the dog's emotion. Understand?"

Sung had thought of the same thing, so he agreed. They walked to Kiukiang, the nearest port where the steamers took on and discharged passengers, but there were no more steamers going up to Hankow that day. Sung spent the rest of the afternoon roving the city, while the circus man led the monkey and the dog out to the dock and the railway station and gave several performances. He told Sung in the evening that he had not earned so much on any other day since they had been on the road.

The following morning the circus man accompanied Sung to the dock, bought the ticket, gave him some extra money, and saw him walk up the

gangplank to the steamship. The excitement of his first river journey helped Sung to live up to his promise as he walked calmly away from the small black dog standing beside the circus man.

The large, freshly painted vessel was filled to capacity, mostly with young men and young women. They were sitting and lying about on the deck, tightly squeezed together. As Sung boarded, many stared at him as if he were a curiosity. Sung found them strange, too—their dress, their accented voices, and their facial expressions. But Sung did not pay too much attention to them, or stare at them as they at him. He was more interested in the steamer. He could not wait but began to inspect it from bow to stern, from smokestack to rudder, picking his way among the crowd, ignoring their vexatious looks. Even the smooth, perfectly round and shining doorknobs intrigued him. He was examining one of them when he felt a hand on his shoulder.

"First time on a steamer?" a tall young man wearing a neatly pressed suit, shining black leather boots, and dark-rimmed spectacles asked in an accented voice.

"Yes," replied Sung.

"From the country?"

"Yes."

"My name is Tang. I boarded the steamer in Shanghai, but my home is in Singapore."

"I know of Shanghai, but where's Singapore?"

"It's a small island country in the South China Sea. But I am Chinese—overseas Chinese, they call

141

us—and a student of Wu-han University. Are you going to Wu-han?"

"To Hankow."

"That's one of the cities of Wu-han. Going to school there?"

"No, to visit my mother. Are all these your schoolmates?"

"Oh, no, I'm all alone on this trip. They are from different schools in Shanghai, being sent to Inner Mongolia to help in farm work and to be reeducated by the farmers." He bent over and whispered in Sung's ear, "Because they made trouble in the city, so you see they are not very happy and won't even speak to me."

Up to that moment, Sung had had some misgivings about Tang. Why, of all the passengers, had he accosted him? Now he understood that the other had no evil intentions but was only lonely, so he spoke to him more freely.

Later in the day, the somber atmosphere on the ship was suddenly broken. Many passengers got up from the deck and shuffled forward, pointing and talking excitedly. Sung looked in the same direction and discovered a hazy, grayish line, like a streak of cloud or smoke, on the far horizon across the broad river. Everyone was talking about the famous Wu-han iron bridge that spans the Yangtze River between Wu-chang and Hankow. It was one of the longest railway bridges in China. As the ship proceeded, the shape of the bridge slowly grew clearer, and its component parts became more discernible. A train came from the north end. It thunderously sucked in the bridge, as it were, and then discharged it from the rear, belching smoke and steam at the same time.

"From Peking," most of the passengers agreed.

"Going to Canton," one said.

"Maybe to Hong Kong," from another.

"No, Chinese trains do not go to Hong Kong, only to Canton," the first one said in an authoritative manner.

The steamer had slowed down as it approached the dock. Tang came over to Sung, caught his elbow, and asked, "Is your mother coming to the pier to meet you, *lao tih*?"

"No, she does not know that I am coming by this steamer," Sung replied. He felt flattered by the way Tang had addressed him as younger brother.

"Where does she live?"

"She works at the First Cotton Mill of Central China in Hankow."

"That's not in Hankow but in Wu-chang, on the south side of the river. How are you going there?"

"Walking."

"But you don't know the way."

"I'll ask."

Tang's handsome face broke into a grin. "That might take you a whole day, or half a day at least. You should hire a pedicab. But it's too late now; the factory will be closed when you get there. Do you have a place to stay tonight?"

"No."

"Well, you cannot sleep in the open. Why don't you come with me? I am going to stay at a small, old-fashioned hotel, named Promotion, only a few hundred paces from the pier. Tomorrow we can catch a ferry and cross the river together; then you can hire a pedicab to the cotton mill, I to the university."

Sung hesitated. He was a little suspicious. But feeling that Tang was sincere, he accepted. However, his suspicion did not completely vanish, especially as Tang insisted on paying all the bills of the hotel and for the meals, until they bid each other good-bye the following morning on the south bank of the river. Then Sung kept repeating to himself, "Yes, there are good people, kind and generous people, who would help others without expecting reward. I only carried his smaller suitcase, but that's not worth one-tenth of the money he spent on me."

It was nearly dark by the time they had checked in at the Promotion Hotel. Sung was anxious to see the city; Tang was no less anxious to show the city to this stranger from the country. So, having gulped down cups of tea, they promptly started out.

The houses they saw were mostly of foreign style, built of red bricks, at least two stories high. The streets were wide, clean, and used mostly by bicycles, pedicabs, automobiles, and carts pulled by men and women, instead of by pedestrians as in the villages. What appeared especially strange to Sung were the glowing furnaces at street corners and beside the houses. At each of these there were people clustering around and drawing the bellows to blow

the fire. Sung wanted to know what they were doing, but he hesitated to ask because he did not want to appear ignorant of so many things. However, the question kept poking him, so finally he blurted it out.

"Don't you know?" Tang replied in a surprised voice. "They are making steel, of course. Haven't you heard of the Great Leap Forward?"

"No, what is that?"

"Chairman Mao wants to speed up China's steel production, so he has ordered everybody to make every effort and utilize every bit of material to make steel. They are doing it in all the large cities. If you go closer to the piles of junk beside the furnaces, you'll see all sorts of things—kitchen utensils, axes, spades, locks, wires, nails, even pocket knives. They are brought in by patriotic people to be melted and

145

made into bars of steel. Now I see why you did not know it. In the countryside, you have a different kind of Great Leap Forward. You don't make steel, but you organize people's communes. Has one been started in your home district?"

"No, not that I know of."

Just then the street lights all came on at the same time without any lamplighters in sight. Sung gasped, but he quickly remembered what Ching Chang had told him about the electric lights in Canton, so he kept his astonishment to himself. Afterward, as he recalled that incident, he congratulated himself that he had not revealed his ignorance yet another time.

20 It had not occurred to Sung that he would be so impatient to see his mother, but now it seemed that the nearer he came to her place and the closer the time for seeing her, the more unbearable became his longing. The morning after his arrival in Hankow, he got up at the break of dawn and aroused Tang from sound sleep.

"I'm sorry to wake you up so early," he apologized, "but I have been awake for a long time, and I must go to see my mother as soon as possible. Somehow I feel that she is anxiously wanting to see me."

"That's all right," Tang mumbled sleepily. "I know how you feel." But he turned over and went to sleep again. Sung waited half a minute, but could not wait any longer. He turned on the electric lamp and called Tang again. Tang obediently got up, rubbed his eyes, and began quickly to dress and pack. In less than five minutes, they were outside the hotel. Tang hailed a pedicab; they climbed in and put the luggage in their laps. Arriving at the ferry dock, they bought fried dough strips, soybean milk, and sticky rice from a snack stall for breakfast, and ate standing like others. They finished just in time to catch the next ferry. It was still early, so passengers were few, and many of them seemed to be travelers with bundles like themselves.

In the middle of the river, Tang took Sung's elbow and led him to the front of the ferry. "Now you can see all the three parts of Wu-han clearly," he said, pointing with his free hand, on the wrist of which was fastened a golden watch. "On the north side of the river is Hankow with its foreign-style houses, because it was once a foreign settlement; on the south side is Wu-chang, a typical, old-fashioned city and a provincial capital; up there on the other side of the Han River is Han-yang, which used to be China's largest steel producing center but is now only one of the largest. At present the three cities are combined into one huge metropolis, named Wu-han. It is one of the most important in China, politically, economically, and militarily. Some people call it the Chicago of China. You don't know Chicago?" He broke into his own monologue, seeing Sung's blank expression. "Well, it's a large city in the United States, also in the heartland of that country, just like Wu-han. Did you know that the first revolution that overthrew the Manchu Dynasty had its start in Wu-chang?"

"Yes, I've heard it." Sung was pleased that he did not give Tang the impression of total ignorance of national affairs.

148

Outside the gate of the pier, Tang hired a pedi-cab for Sung before he hired one for himself. When Sung had been comfortably seated in the cab, Tang held out his hand to bid him good-bye and said, "You'll be seeing your mother in an hour or so. Hope you'll have a good time. Please come to visit my university with her one of these days." He turned to the cabman and added, "He's very anxious to see his mother, so please pedal as fast as you can."

The pedicab quickly picked up speed. After five

or six minutes, the cabman opened his shirt and pedaled so fast that the sides of the shirt flew and flapped madly. Sung wanted to ask him to slow down a bit, because the speed frightened him. He thought the cab might overturn or hit someone or something. In just about an hour the cab stopped outside an arched, iron-grated gate in the high brick wall that surrounded a large factory with a tall chimney. Sung got off and counted out the fare. Then he went up to a guard who wore a gray soldier's uniform and carried a rifle.

The guard took Sung to a small room inside the gate and left him to an older man wearing heavy glasses. This was the gateman. He took the register book out of the desk drawer and asked Sung to write his name and the name of the person he wanted to visit. Sung did as he was told. The gateman brought the book close to his eyes and peered at it; then he said animatedly, "So *you* are the boy to visit your mother—but she has gone!"

"Gone! Where has she gone?" Sung cried.

"She has been expecting you for a long time. She came to the gate to inquire every day, several times a day, whether you had come. But she has gone."

"Where?" Sung repeated.

"Gone home. To join the people's commune and the Great Leap Forward."

"But we have no home. It's been occupied by other people."

"Yes, she has gone home; she told me herself," the

man insisted. "She would take a steamer to Kiukiang, change to the train, then hire a wheelbarrow —I tell you what!" The gateman's thin face suddenly beamed in excitement. "She left just about two hours ago; maybe she's still at the dock. Maybe the steamer has not yet gone."

Sung jumped up from the bench and ran out of the gate. He looked for a pedicab but there were none. He remembered the general direction from which he had come, so he started to run. He ran as fast as his breath could take him. Ten or fifteen minutes later, he saw a ricksha and hired it to the ferry dock. He arrived when a ferry was waiting, and just had time to dash into the palisaded gate before it closed.

On the ferry he saw nothing, heard nothing, and was aware of nothing. His mind was completely occupied by one thought—to reach the pier before the steamer left with his mother. He was one of the first passengers off the ferry. He dashed to the pier, but even before he arrived he saw that no steamer was anchored there. He asked and found out that the boat to Kiukiang had left more than an hour earlier.

Sung sighed heavily and felt like crying, but no tears would come to his eyes. He sat down at the edge of the pier and wiped his face and neck. He was too confused to think clearly. Then gradually it dawned on him that the student had given him bad advice. He blamed himself for having listened. He should have come to the factory yesterday. Even if

151

it had been closed, he could have waited outside; then he would have met his mother this morning.

"Oh, what bad luck!" Sung thought. He had left Lucky, so luck had left him. What should he do now that he was all alone and so far from home? Where were Lucky and the circus man? He had no idea, and there was no possibility of finding them. Then he thought of going to the university to see Tang and borrow some money. Tang was rich and generous, so surely he would lend enough money for the trip home. But who knew how far it was to the university?

He had no money to hire a pedicab; no money to pay for the ferry. "What can I do? Oh, Heaven, what can I do?" thought Sung. He held his head in both hands and rested his elbows on his knees, and remained quiet.

It was as though Heaven answered his question, for in less than a minute he remembered the money Ching Chang's wife had sewed inside the pocket of his jacket. He opened the pocket and the bag with his teeth, to make sure the money was still there. Yes, it was! He squeezed the money in his palm, and wanted to cry and dance for joy. "How wise is Aunt Ching Chang! What foresight! What a guardian angel!" he said of the pig dealer's wife.

Then Sung realized that going home was no problem as long as he had the money. He had been told many times before he set out on the journey how to go to Hankow by train and steamer—to walk about half a day to the railroad station, ride a train to Kiukiang, then change to the steamer. To go home from Hankow, he would simply reverse the order of travel.

His problem solved, Sung had nothing to worry about or to do but to wait till the following morning to board the steamer to Kiukiang. He spent the afternoon roaming the streets of Hankow and inspecting the manufacture of steel of the Great Leap Forward. He passed by a large restaurant. Inside the wide show window were displayed trays of various exotic pastries. They looked delicious. Sung's mouth watered as he stood there watching and admiring, but he could not summon up sufficient courage to go inside. They might be expensive; they must be; the waiter might even turn him out. He bought a bowl of cold noodles seasoned with sesame oil and red peppers for supper. He thought of lodging in the Promotion Hotel, but that also was expensive. So he slept beside a furnace for making steel; it was warm and comfortable compared to what he had experienced on his last trip, when he roved the villages in search of Lucky.

Sung boarded the steamer to Kiukiang the following morning. It was the same steamer that had brought him to Hankow. In Kiukiang he got off and walked to the railroad station, and spent the night there sleeping on a bench.

He reached New Market Place, his home town, at noon the third day. He was not sure that his mother had arrived or where she would be staying. He decided he would go to Ching Chang's home to find out. As he came to New Market Place, he saw many people pouring into Yui-wang-kung temple, so he followed the crowd through the familiar, stone-framed gate. The spacious courtyard was nearly filled, and there were many more people up on the terrace, which had contained the shrines and statues, now removed. The coffins, too, had been removed, and in their places were more people.

Up on the stage, right inside the entrance, there were many rattan chairs, wooden chairs, and benches, which were empty.

Sung asked an elderly man, who wore a skullcap and a dilapidated satin jacket, what was going to

happen. The man stared at Sung in astonishment and replied, "You don't know about the Great Leap Forward? We are going to organize the people's commune. That is what's happening here."

Sung remembered what the university student Tang and the gateman at the factory had told him in Wu-han. "So it's true," he thought. "We are getting started at home."

Just then, a column of men and women emerged from the back of the stage. Leading the way was a smallish young man in a new blue tunic. Something about him struck Sung as familiar. The boy tried to recall where he had seen him before. Ah, the commissar, he remembered, who had come to New Market Place some months ago and launched the Annihilate-the-Dogs Campaign at the teahouse. The next familiar figure Sung noticed was Ching Chang, a massive form, also in a new tunic and more dignified than ever. Before he had enough time to admire Ching Chang, he had, to his unutterable astonishment, caught sight of his mother! Why was she on stage with the commissar? What did it all mean?

As Sung puzzled, the town crier came to the front of the stage and shouted in a shrill voice to the audience to be quiet. When the hubbub had subsided, he introduced the commissar. The diminutive but grave-looking young man shuffled slowly to the middle front of the stage and planted himself behind a table, on which was spread a sheet of white cloth, a teapot, and two cups. He scanned the audience and remained silent for about half a minute; then

156

coughed and began:

"Today is the most important and most memorable day in the history of New Market Place, and I am pleased to see such an enthusiastic crowd present. We are the first in this district of ours to leap forward to the socialist society and create the people's commune. 'What is the people's commune?' you ask. Simply that several thousand individual families—farmers, artisans, merchants, teachers, etc. —combine into one large unit, like one family. From now on, we shall work together, help each other, and enjoy the result of our labors together. Our fields and plows, water buffaloes and oxen will belong to all of us, not to individuals. We will plant our rice and corn and beans and other crops in teams; we will cultivate them in teams, and cut the weeds in teams. Most of us, of course, will work in the fields, but some of us will undertake other kinds of labor—carpentering, blacksmithing, brick-making, tailoring, sewing, and so on . . ." He continued to enumerate the benefits of the commune for some time, but Sung's mind had wandered away. He had to speak to his mother, find out if she had heard from his father, and where she was staying.

The commissar had finished. He began to introduce the other personages. One of the first to be presented was Ching Chang, the expert on swine, under whose charge all the pigs of the commune would be placed. Toward the end of the list, Sung's mother was introduced; she would take charge of the tailor shops of the commune. She was smiling

157

and Sung was pleased. Just then Sung noticed a short ladder at one side of the stage. He could make use of that, if he could only get to it. He started to move in that direction, elbowing, squeezing, worming, apologizing, and keeping his head bent. At last he reached the ladder. The commissar started as he leaped onto the stage, and there was a minor commotion. But the man was soon put at ease, as Sung ran up to his mother and threw his arms around her.

Hugging him, she took him at once to the back of the stage and asked him, "Where have you been?"

"In Wu-han. I went to your cotton mill, but you had just left. I was also at Po-yang looking for Father, but there were so many people there I could not find him."

His mother held him closer, and a tear dropped onto his head. "I know," she said.

"Where are you staying?" Sung asked, hoping to cheer her.

"Ching Chang's wife invited me to stay there last night but I am going home tonight," she replied, motioning toward some bundles piled up at the side of the stage.

"But our home has been occupied by other people."

"They've moved out and the house has been returned to us," she assured him.

"But there is nothing left."

Then Sung remembered his mother's hairpin. He groped in his pocket anxiously, as though afraid that it might no longer be there; then his face beamed as his fingers found the object of his search. He presented it to her with both hands, and she gasped and said, "Why, you have not sold it!" She pressed it to her cheek, and quickly arranged it in her hair. Then she asked about Lucky, and Sung whispered the story to her, as the program for the people's commune continued.

The sun had gone down when the rally finally ended and the people poured from the temple into the street. They gathered in clusters and talked about the changes that were to take place. Sung and his mother clung together and started for home, Sung helping her to carry her bundles.

When they reached the edge of the family threshing yard, a few stars were visible above the shaddock tree. They stopped beneath the tree to look at their house. It had an abandoned appearance, the doors standing ajar and swinging in the evening breeze.

Sung hurried ahead and ran up the steps, entering the house before his mother. The rooms were strewn with pieces of newspapers and torn pages of books, cigarette butts, and burned matches. In the kitchen a small pile of dry twigs and straw lay before the stone-and-mud stove, and the large earthen jar was half full of clear water. Sung's mother took a tallow candle and a box of matches from her parcel and lit the candle. At once she started to build a fire in the stove with the twigs and straw and to heat the rice that Ching Chang's thoughtful wife had persuaded her to accept.

They ate supper standing before the stove. Tomorrow they would go to Ching Chang to borrow a table and a couple of benches.

When Sung at last rolled himself up in the quilt his mother gave him, he could see her in the doorway, gazing out across the starlit fields. All was quiet. No dog barked. In the stillness, Sung heard his mother sigh. He wanted to comfort her, though he knew he could not.

Far away in New Market Place a few firecrackers popped, and Sung knew some people were still celebrating the Great Leap Forward. He wondered if the new program had gotten underway at Po-yang Lake, or wherever his father was now. He felt a great loneliness, thinking of his father, and could only hope that someday he, too, would come home.

But Lucky could never come home. Sung buried his face deep in the quilt. There was no use to think of that. At least he had saved Lucky. Every day he could take comfort in the thought that the little dog was performing somewhere, endlessly circling, pulling the tiny plow while the monkey held the whip.